THE GARDEN

AMY SPARLING

CHAPTER ONE

MY INSTAGRAM FEED is filled with snow-covered landscapes and elite socialites all bundled up in Gucci sweaters and knee-high boots posing with their pumpkin spice lattes in hand. To all that winter aesthetic stuff, I say: *gross*.

In many parts of the world, January is a frigid, snowy awful month of warm layers, electric blankets, scraping ice off your car, and eating hot soup or whatever it is people do in cold climates. But here in sunny California, it is an absolutely perfect seventy degrees. (Or twenty-one degrees Celsius, as my Canadian chef likes to say.)

I look away from my phone, letting my head fall back on the lounge chair, my eyes closing while I listen to the sound of the pool water sloshing through the filter, and feel the warm sun on my face. The Malibu mansion is truly my favorite of all our homes. We used to only come here in the summers, but as soon as I got old enough to start calling the shots, I settled down in our Malibu vacation home and let my parents go wherever they wanted to go for the rest of the year. Sure, Cali isn't as historic as England or as gorgeous as Thailand, but I feel a sense of belonging here.

My phone starts ringing the cheerful Shawn Mendes song I've assigned as my best friend Viv's ring tone. Well – she's a *close* friend. You don't exactly have best friends in the traditional sense when your family is wealthier than everyone else's. You really never know who you can trust and who is trying to use you for your connections. I'm pretty sure that everyone is trying to use you when you're rich.

But Viv's mom is the president of a large fashion company, so they're doing pretty well with money. I trust her for the most part.

"Hey," I say, putting the phone to my ear as I relax by the pool.

"There's another MTV party tonight," she says, heaving a sigh like it took a lot of energy to get out those words. "Are we going? I'm kind of tired of the music scene."

That's probably because her beloved Shawn Mendes hasn't noticed that she exists yet, despite her pretty desperate attempts to flirt with him. But I'm not going to say it out loud. Girl code and all that.

"I'm over the music scene, too," I say. Solidarity. Truth is, any party is my scene right now. As long as I'm not stuck at home for another awkward dinner with my parents who are staying here this summer, I don't care where I am. I love my mom and dad, but they're basically strangers lately.

"Great," Viv says. "We'll find something else to do."

The clickity-clack sound of Charlie's heels draws my attention to where my mom's assistant is approaching from across the pool. She waves frantically at me like it's important.

"Viv? I'll call you back."

"Kay, but don't forget. You always forget."

I roll my eyes and promise that I won't forget. But now that the MTV party is out tonight, I have no idea what else would top that. I haven't posted to Instagram in a few days and my adoring followers will want to see something that makes them envious. That's why they follow me, after all.

"Sophia," Charlie says, smiling politely at me as her tall frame hovers over mine. She works for my mom full time, and she basically lives here, but she doesn't dress like it. She only ever wears pant suits or blazers and matching skirts. And always heels. I mean, props to the woman for wearing heels twenty-four hours a day, but holy crap, the fancy clothing must get old. I practically live in my jeans, leggings, and oversized shirts. The ironic thing is that my designer loungewear costs ten times what her formal work clothes cost.

"What's up?" I say, peering up at her. She's in her early thirties, but easily looks as stressed as a fifty-year-old heart surgeon. You can blame that on my mom, who asks a lot out of the poor woman.

"You'll need to pack up your things, hon." She glances at the tablet in her hand, and something tells me she just doesn't want to meet my eye. "Your plane is leaving in the morning."

"Where am I going?"

She checks the tablet again. "Some small town in New England."

"New England?" There is nothing cool in that part of the country. In fact, it's one of those places that gets snowy and gross in the winter. I am absolutely not going there.

Charlie nods. "Your flight is at ten-thirty. Mrs. Brass has informed me that you'll be attending school there until you graduate, so pack enough clothes and belongings for the duration."

"*What?*" I fling my sunglasses off and stand up. I am

equal parts confused and angry. No wait, strike that—I am mostly angry, and only a little bit confused.

Of course my mom would send her lackey to tell me upsetting news. She always does. Mom doesn't say anything herself unless it makes her look good.

I storm past Charlie and into the house, my bare feet cold on the white marble floors. "Mom!" I call out, even though it's loud and rude and everything my mother hates. "Where are you?"

"Calm down, child," Mom says in a voice that's stern and unaffected, aka-her normal voice.

Charlie is right on my heels, no doubt clutching that tablet and thinking of excuses to placate my mom. I'm sure if my mom had it her way, she'd never have to speak to me.

"What is all this talk about me flying out to New England tomorrow? Is this some kind of joke? Because I'm not laughing."

My mother is beautiful, starkly put together, and absolutely as cold and unfeeling as the stone tiles beneath my feet.

She glances up from the book she's reading, her dark brown eyes meeting mine for the first time in weeks. We might live in the same house a few months a year, but we mostly communicate through Charlie, or text message.

"Your grades have become unacceptable ever since you started partying more than you study."

I scoff. "I don't really have grades, Mom." My private tutors teach me lessons three days a week and I do assignments and they never give me grades. That's how it's always been, and that's how it is for all of my friends who are also homeschooled with private tutors.

"You know what I mean," she says, glancing back at her book. "You're not dedicating yourself to school, and you need to because this is supposed to be your senior year. I refuse to be the next face of a college admission scandal, so you better believe I'm not paying off a college to accept you. You'll have to get in on grades alone."

"I don't really care about college," I say.

"If you want your trust fund, you'll go to college."

That shuts me up. My trust fund kicks in when I turn twenty-one. It's enough money to allow me to do whatever I want for the rest of my life. And all I have to do is attend some stupid college for four years to get it. I take a deep breath and try another approach.

"I apologize about slacking in my schoolwork. I'll ask my tutors for extra credit and I'll work harder."

Mom's head shakes one time in a sharp, precise no. "You're leaving tomorrow. You've been enrolled in Shelfbrooke Academy and you will finish out this semester with a group of your peers. They've agreed to let you take the standardized tests and graduate with a diploma, if you just put in the work."

"Shelfbrooke Academy? Where have I heard that name before?"

I have very little to do with the east coast, so I'm pretty sure I haven't dated anyone from there or been to one of their parties while visiting our NYC home.

Mom flips the page in her book. "My sister lives there."

Oh. The air whooshes out of me. "You're sending me to school with my cousin Belle?"

"She does attend that school," Mom says.

I groan. Belle and I are the same age. We were friends when we were little kids, but quickly grew apart. Something about my aunt choosing not to accept the monumental inheritance from my grandmother when she passed away. I don't remember the story, just that my mom and her sister fought very loudly after the funeral and then I never saw either one of them again.

"Mom, please don't do this to me."

"It's already done."

"Mom, please."

"Don't whine, Sophia, it's an awful look on you."

I grit my teeth. I hate when she makes me feel stupid. My mom is not the touchy-feely type. If anything, her assistant Charlie is more of a mom than my own mom.

I take a deep breath and shove all the things I want to say to the back of my mind. Not because I'm trying to be a good daughter or anything, but because I don't want to give my mom the satisfaction of seeing me angry.

"Guess I'm going to Shelfbend Academy."

"Shelf*brooke*," Mom corrects, her eyes on her book.

"Shelfbrooke," I say, mostly to myself so I can remember this stupid school's name. I want to go back out to the pool and Google and it see exactly what my parents have gotten me into.

I sweep past Charlie and her concerned expression and walk right back outside to our rooftop pool, pretending for all to see that I have no problems at all. I am Sophia Brass, and I don't have a care in the world. I find my phone sitting in the lounge chair from where it had fallen when I abruptly left a few minutes ago. I pick it up and press a button, then hold into my ear.

"Viv?" I say when she answers. "Told you I'd call you back. We have a problem. A huge, life-shattering problem."

"Oohh," Viv says, and I can practically feel her eyebrows wiggling mischievously even though she lives a mile down the beach. The girl loves a good bit of drama. "I'll be right over."

CHAPTER TWO

SITTING by the pool is not as much fun when I'm fuming mad. I stretch out my legs on the lounge chair and I close my eyes and let the sunshine warm my face and I take deep, deep, yoga breaths.

It does nothing to help.

I am so mad I wouldn't be surprised if flames suddenly shot out of my eyes. How could my parents do this to me? They've spent most of my life completely ignoring me and letting me do whatever I wanted while under the loose supervision of nannies. Now suddenly they care about my education? This is crap!

Viv arrives a few minutes later, her eyes wide and mischievous because she loves a good gossip, or tea-spilling as she likes to say. The second she walks onto the rooftop patio, her Givenchy flip flops smacking the pavement, wavy bleach blonde hair swaying beautifully behind her, I don't feel relieved to see her. In fact, I get the same feeling I normally get when I'm around her for too long, although it usually takes about an hour for that feeling to kick in.

The truth is... I kind of hate my best friend.

I mean, she's fun and beautiful and our parents are friends and we're in all the same socialite friendship circles, but deep down in the very center of my heart, I can't stand her. I can't stand a lot of things about my life, but every time I've even dared to mention it, Charlie will tell me to stop being a brat and be grateful for my awesome life.

I grit my teeth, force back my secret hatred of my best friend and wave at her as she approaches. I get up and hug her, then we sit next to each other on the lounge chairs.

"Spill," she says, tipping her sunglasses down from the top of her head. "Are your parents getting divorced?"

"What?" I roll my eyes and stare out at the pool. "No."

"Oh," she says, sounding surprised. "Well, that's good. What happened?"

I heave a sigh and find that it's harder to say the words than I imagined. It feels icky, embarrassing. Like I have to confess that I've kissed a poor guy or something.

"My parents have gone completely insane and they've decided to pull me out of private tutoring in the middle of my senior year and send me to a freaking boarding school."

Viv's shoulders fall. "That's it?"

"What do you mean 'that's it'? This is terrible news!"

She chews on her bottom lip for a second and then smiles at me. "Sophia, it's really not a big deal. I mean, there's like four months of school left, right? We'll still hang out every day and party every night. It'll be fine."

"No, because I won't be here in California."

She sits up straighter. "You're going away?"

I nod, happy that she's finally looking concerned.

"But why?" she says. "There are tons of great boarding schools here in Cali."

I shrug. "Like I said, my parents have gone insane. Maybe I could get myself emancipated due to their insanity."

Viv chuckles. "You're forgetting the number one rule of rich kids."

"And that is?"

She looks at me like I'm dumb. "Hello? Your trust fund? Our parents use them to control us?"

I groan and lean back against my chair, covering my face with my hands. She's right. She's totally right. Right now I live on my parent's dime. My trust fund is big enough to keep me set for life, but I don't get it until I'm twenty one. Viv's parents are even worse, because they're making her get a college degree before she has access to her trust fund. That means we're still stuck doing whatever our parents want until we're old enough to get our money. That means if my parents told me to dress like a clown every day for a week, I'd have to do it.

That means I have to go to boarding school.

"So where is it?" Viv asks.

"Shelfbrooke."

"Oh!" She perks up and gives me a reassuring pat on the arm. "That's not so bad. It's a pretty prestigious school. Lots of future congressman attend Shelfbrooke. The D'Villes go there, too."

"Yeah but it's on the east coast. Only losers live on the east coast."

Viv laughs. I get the feeling she's enjoying my pain a little too much. Shouldn't a real best friend be here for me, suffering and freaking out too?

"It's just a few months, Soph. I'll still be here when you get back."

"Our summer plans are still on, okay? I refuse to let my parents' stupid new rule derail that."

"Oh, it is so on," she says with a grin. "Europe won't know what to do with us."

I smile too, happy that, for all her faults, my best friend is still my best friend. And maybe I can just get through these next few months, graduate, and then come back home where I belong. And Viv and I can go on our senior trip that we've planned for years. We're going to charter a private jet and see all of Europe in style. It's like a wealthy persons' take on the old "backpacking around Europe" dream. We're going to do it in style.

"It's just a few months," I say, taking a deep breath to calm my nerves.

"It's just a few months," Viv repeats.

"Knock, knock," a voice says from behind us. My heart immediately swells with anticipation. The voice belongs to Henry Sharp. *The* Henry Sharp, of the Sharp congressman legacy. His dad is gearing up for his presidential run, and Henry plans to follow in his footsteps.

We've been getting close lately, flirting over text and in person. If I play my cards right, I might become a future First Lady. I think I would look really, really good in front of the White House.

"Henry!" I say, getting up and giving him a hug. "I didn't know you were coming over."

He shrugs, that boyish grin making my stomach flutter. Henry has it all. He's tall, toned, and absolutely gorgeous. His family moved to Malibu after his dad became a senator. All the girls immediately threw themselves at him, but I feel like Henry and I have a connection. Maybe because I'm smart enough to act confident around him. It's a much better look than desperation.

"I saw your Snaps," he says, referencing the Snapchat pictures I posted a little while ago. I was happy back then because it was before my mother dropped the boarding school bomb on me. Henry smiles and runs a hand through his dirty blond hair. "Thought I'd surprise you."

"Well it's good timing because you won't be seeing her for a while," Viv says. I stiffen and give her a glare she doesn't seem to notice. I wanted to be the one to tell him, not her.

Henry frowns. "What do you mean?"

"She's being sent off to boarding school."

Now his brows shoot up and then he grins. "You're joking, right? It's the middle of the year."

I throw my hands up in the air. "Tell that to my parents. They're sending me away tomorrow because they want me to get good grades at an actual school instead of from my private tutors."

"That's harsh," he says. "Where are you going?"

"Shelfbrooke."

He grimaces. "That's far away."

I lean my head on his shoulder. "I know," I say with a heavy sigh.

He pats my back but it does nothing to comfort me. "Let's swim. Take your mind off it."

I know I should suck it up and go swim with him. He's Henry Sharp after all. But my stomach hurts and I'm feeling dizzy from the realization that I'll be leaving tomorrow morning. I shake my head. "You swim. I just need to sit down."

"I'll swim with you!" Viv says, eagerly stripping off her sheer coverup and revealing the hot pink bikini she wears underneath.

"Cool," Henry says with that gorgeous smile of his. He reaches out his hand and my best friend takes it, knowing full well that I have claimed Henry as my own crush, and together they jump into my pool.

I guess I should have seen this coming. Tomorrow I'll be gone. Out of the picture. Shipped off to the stupid east coast. But my best friend and Henry will still be here, living it up in Malibu.

I watch the sun glistening off Viv's gorgeous wet hair. I hear the sound of her laughter as Henry splashes her. Then the sound of his laughter as she splashes him back. And just like that, my future First Lady plans are ripped out from under me.

I think I'm going to be sick.

CHAPTER THREE

MY HAND WRAPS around the handles of my Prada suitcases. Three more suitcases are being overnighted to the boarding school, filled with my clothing and belongings. This one is my carry on. It didn't feel real when I was packing last night, but it feels real now. It feels real like a sucker punch to the gut.

I didn't even say goodbye to my parents this morning because they were already gone, headed off to Bali for some "marriage counseling" which we all know is just a fancy way to say you're spending a lot of money getting pampered at a resort. They couldn't be bothered to tell me goodbye when their plane left last night, and I won't be bothered to text them goodbye now, as I stand at my front door, watching the driver pull up and get out, opening the back door for me.

I take a deep breath. I walk down the front steps of my Malibu house, knowing I will count every single day until I get to come back here where I belong.

"Good morning, Miss Brass," the driver says. I don't know his name. I give him a slight nod, which is all I can muster right now. It's really freaking early in the morning and I am being relocated against my will. I can't bother to smile right now.

The drive to the airport is short. We go to a private air strip just a few minutes away, where the chartered jet is waiting for us. My parents own a third of the jet and share it with two other prominent families. Today I get to use it.

The private jet is fun, but now when you're being flown to a stuffy pathetic boarding school. Ugh.

I can't believe my parents are doing this to me!

I normally try to sleep on planes because I get nervous from the turbulence, but today I am wide awake. My stomach is in knots, and I can't even drink the orange juice that comes with my in-flight breakfast, and that's saying something because I love orange juice. In just a few hours I'll be deposited at Shelfbrooke Academy and I don't even know what to do once I get there. Charlie's notes in my email say my Aunt Kate will pick me up. But I'm not sure I can remember what she looks like. It's been a long time.

I can't believe my parents are doing this to me. I keep hoping this is some kind of cruel joke, a prank my very well-mannered parents decided to do just to get a laugh. Even though that's not like them at all, I still hold onto the hope. I keep expecting them to pop out from the back cabin in the plane and yell "Got you!" and laugh and laugh and say it was all just a joke.

But, of course, that doesn't happen.

Viv told me I should make a big deal about my moving away on Snapchat, but I decided against it. I made her swear not to tell anyone that I'm leaving. Maybe I can just disappear mysteriously for a few months and people will wonder where I am. It can be an interesting secret and it'll make my California friends eager to see me again. Maybe I'll get even more popular from this. So long as Viv keeps her promise. Now that she has Henry in her sights, she probably won't be thinking about me at all.

The plane lands way sooner than I want it to. Touching down on the New England runway means I'm here. It means my Malibu life is halted, put on hold for several months. It means everything is going to change, and not in a good way like when you get a nose job.

These changes suck.

I grab my suitcase and shuffle down the fold out stairs and onto the tarmac. Inside the small private airport, a few people mull around. None of them look like my aunt. I chew on the inside of my lip, checking my phone, hoping someone has sent me some kind of instructions on what to do. But Charlie has left me on my own, it seems.

About ten minutes go by, with me standing here feeling out of place for the first time in my life, and finally I see a tall guy wearing skinny jeans and a plaid jacket, walking around like he's looking for someone. We make eye contact.

"Sophia Brass?"

"Yes," I say, relief flooding over me. "Are you my ride?"

"Yes ma'am," he says, gesturing for me to follow him. "My car is right out here."

I quickly discover that when he said *car*, he meant car. Like a regular car.

I frown as he puts my suitcase into the trunk and I climb into the backseat, noticing the rideshare logo stuck to the window. This is a ride share car. Not a private car. I've never been in a rideshare car in my life. That's something people without trust funds do. Ugh.

The guy is polite, but he likes to talk, and it's annoying. The drive takes forever, but soon he's pulling into the driveway of some kind of old apartment complex. The red bricks match all the other houses we've driven by, and there's a large gate around the parking lot, all covered with vines. But this is clearly an apartment complex, not a school. At least –gosh—I hope this isn't the school.

"Where are we?" I ask.

"Umm, your destination?" he says, checking his phone. "Kate's home?"

I laugh. "Ah. Okay. Cool."

This isn't my new school.

I waiver for a minute, wondering if I'm supposed to tip him. I mean, probably, right? I reach in my purse and take out a hundred-dollar bill and hand it over. "Thank you for driving me."

His eyes bug out, then he holds up his hand. "I can't accept that."

"Why not?" I hold it out to him again. "I'm tipping you. That's what people do with rideshares, right?"

He grins, and little wrinkles form in the crease of his eyes. He dresses like he's twenty, but he's probably closer to forty. "Ms. Kate has already tipped me through the app."

"Oh," I say, feeling my cheeks flush. I shrug. "Well, take it anyway, please. It's my parents' money if it makes you feel any better."

He stares at the hundred-dollar bill for a long

moment and then he finally takes it. "Thank you. I appreciate it."

I get out of the car and stare up at the large building in front of me. There are five front doors, five sidewalks going up to them, and five numbers on each door. I have no idea which one belongs to my Aunt Kate. I turn around to ask the driver if he knows, but he's already pulling out of the parking lot. Great. Just great.

Charlie's one and only email just told me some information about my new school. I'd ignored it because I was angry, but maybe it has my aunt's address on it.

I pull out my phone and scroll through the email. Sure enough, it does. It even says I should look for an Uber driver at the airport. Oops. Maybe I should have read this.

Aunt Kate's condo is the third one. My heart pounds in my chest as I walk up to it. Why do I feel so sick? Why do I feel like the sky is falling and my life is ending? It's only a few months, I remind myself. This will be okay. I'll survive.

I knock on the door.

A woman who looks a lot like my mom appears on the other side. "Sophia! Look at you!" she says, holding out her arms for a hug. "Absolutely stunning!"

I lean into her, hugging my aunt for the first time in

years. Her resemblance to my mom is uncanny, but it's like they were raised on different planets. Mom is thin, toned, tanned, and always wearing a perfect face of makeup. She gets weekly Botox injections, and bi-weekly hair appointments. My aunt is, well, not that. She's wrinkly, with gray hairs poking out from her brown locks. She has a little pudge on her stomach, and her nails are unpainted. Her ears devoid of jewelry. But even I have to admit, she looks a lot nicer than my mom. She looks friendly. Caring. Motherly.

"How was your trip?" she asks.

"It was okay." I glance around the living room. The furniture is old. The couches are floral print. There are tons of knickknacks and plants everywhere. My aunt's living room looks like something you'd see in an old grandma's house on television. It's not horrible or messy or anything, just not what I'm used to. The air smells like chocolate chip cookies though, and I can get behind that.

"Where's Belle?"

"Oh, she's at school," she says. "I had to pull some strings, but I got you in her dorm! Isn't that great? You won't have to share with a stranger."

"The dorms are shared?" I say, curling my lip.

My aunt laughs. "For the most part, yes. Some people are lucky enough to have a private room. Belle's roommate left in her freshman year and she got moved to a new room. She's had the room all to herself since then."

"I don't want to impose," I say. "Maybe they could find another empty room for me?"

She laughs again. "Honey, if that were possible, don't you think your mom would have paid for one by now?"

I roll my eyes at the mention of my mom. "I don't know what she would do. She clearly hates me for sending me here."

"Oh, it's not so bad," Aunt Kate says. "You'll get a great education. You want some cookies? I have a fresh batch in the kitchen. You can take the rest with you to Belle."

My brain feels overworked. Like it's thinking way too hard, like when I'm trying to work out a complicated calculus problem. And it's all because I just realized I'll be living in a dorm. I guess I knew that, deep down, that boarding schools mean dorms, but it hadn't sunk in until now. Rooming with my cousin should be better in theory, but she isn't even my friend. Hopefully she's cool. Maybe if I sweet-talk some people in charge, I'll be able to get my own room. Or, maybe I can just rent an apartment off campus. That would be perfect. When I mention this last idea to my aunt, she bursts out laughing.

"Honey, they don't allow students to live off-campus. You have to live in a dorm."

"Great. Just great."

"You'll be fine," Aunt Kate says. "Here, have a cookie."

I eat two of the chocolate chip cookies, which are still delightfully warm from the oven, and then my aunt packs the rest up in a plastic container. We get in her car, which is an old Ford SUV thing that has seen better days. I try not to look disgusted. I don't know why my aunt didn't take the family money, but she should have. She could be living a much better life than this one with a crappy car and old, small condo. I have no idea how she even affords the tuition for Belle's schooling.

My aunt chatters away on the drive to the school. It takes exactly two minutes. I didn't realize she lived so close. Now my nerves are on overdrive. I'm practically on fire with how freaked out I am as we drive up to Shelfbrooke Academy. The campus grounds are huge, over five hundred acres my aunt says, and they're all contained behind an ancient stone wall. At the entrance, the wall becomes an old stone gate, which we drive through. It looks a lot like the New England ivy league schools, with ancient campus buildings and beautiful old trees, and worn stone pathways connecting them all.

The only difference is that all the students on campus are wearing a uniform.

My aunt drives right up to a building and puts the

car in park. "So it's just down that hallway, to the right. Belle's dorm is number sixty-two. She's expecting you. I have to get to work or I'd walk you inside," she says, looking over at me. Then she frowns. "You okay? You know what, I'll go inside if you want."

I shake my head and swallow down my nerves. The last thing I want to do is be brought inside with a parent like I'm some kind of pathetic little kid.

"It's fine," I say, offering her the best smile I can muster. "I'll be fine."

Aunt Kate smiles and squeezes my hand. She seems to believe me. I really wish I believed myself.

CHAPTER FOUR

IT'S JUST after eleven in the morning, and I don't see any other students as I walk toward the dorm, rolling my suitcases behind me. There were students walking around when we drove in, but this part of the campus is deserted. You would think that dorm rooms would be filled with people bustling around, but maybe I'm just projecting my love of Gilmore Girls onto reality. Maybe in reality, everyone is in class right now.

Still, my heart pounds and my palms feel sweaty. I've never been so horribly out of place in my life. I pull open the door to the building where my aunt had told me to go. Inside, the floors are made of gray marble that looks as ancient as the rest of the building. The left side of the hallway is just a wall with no windows. Framed portraits of important old people line the walls, as well as a bulletin board, and some other plaques. On the right side of the hallway are a bunch of doors. The numbers start at forty. I stand straight, tell myself I'm Sophia Brass, I'm extremely wealthy and popular, and well liked. I can handle this. I walk forward, counting off the doors as the numbers slowly increase, until finally, I'm at number sixty-two. It's a little frightening how short the distance is between each door. I'm imagining a room the size of a closet when I knock on the ancient wooden door in front of me, the numbers 62 on it in gold embossed numbers.

Several seconds go by and nothing happens. I knock again, louder this time. Maybe the old wooden door is so thick she can't hear me knocking. Again, nothing.

"Belle?" I call out, pressing my face close to the door. "Are you in there? It's Sophia."

The sound of a deadbolt clicks, and then the door slowly opens. A girl's face appears in the slight open width of the door. It's Belle. At least I think it is.

"Belle?"

Her dark eyes are wide. She looks frightened, or at the very least, freaked out.

"It's me," I say, smiling. "Sophia? Your cousin?"

"I know," she says, her voice whisper-soft. She pulls open the door further, and steps back to let me inside. "Are you alone?"

"Yeah. Aunt Kate had to go to work so she dropped me off."

The second I'm inside the dorm room, Belle closes the door and twists the deadbolt back into place. Then she turns to face me. My cousin is a little taller than I am, willowy, and pale. Her long dark hair goes all the way to her waist, falling in unkept soft waves down her shoulders. She's wearing black leggings and a red sweater, with black and red plaid house shoes on her feet.

"How are you?" she asks, a soft smile tipping up on her lips.

If I didn't know any better, I'd think my frail-looking cousin was suffering some disease. She's so tiny and fragile. Wait...

Maybe she is. I don't know anything about her.

"I'm fine," I say, smiling again. "How are you? Are you okay?"

She nods quickly, her hand tugging at the sleeve of her other arm. "I'm good." She holds her hands out. "Welcome to the dorm."

I take this opportunity to look around. The room is narrow, but it's not quite the size of a closet, to my relief. This part of the dorm is a living area, with two small loveseats, a coffee table, and a low bookshelf that's filled with books, both of the textbook variety and of the fun, fictional variety. Then further down the narrow room, two beds are up against each corner. There are identical bookshelves next to each bed, but one is empty. Between the beds against the far wall, is a very tall window that stretches from a few feet above the floor and goes all the way up to the high ceilings. I look up, taking in the sight of the tall ceilings, which seems to make the room feel bigger. The bed on the right is clearly Belle's because it's made up with purple sheets and tons of pillows. Posters of classic literary novels line the walls. The bookshelf next to her bed is filled with more books and storage boxes.

My bed has a bare mattress, no pillows, and a stack of uniforms.

I roll my suitcases to the bed and run my fingers over the uniforms. "Are these mine?"

Belle nods. "The laundry crew drops them off each Tuesday, all fresh and clean."

"These are hideous. But at least everyone has to wear them," I say with a snort.

Belle's smile fades away. "So obviously, this is your bed. You should get some new sheets as soon as you can. The stuff they supply here is awful and scratchy. I can let you borrow some of my sheets for now. That's your closet," she says pointing to a narrow door to the left of my bed. "And that's the bathroom."

I pull open the other door and peer inside what is the smallest bathroom I've ever seen. There's just a shower, toilet, and small sink.

"This is totally not okay," I say, closing the door and turning back to my cousin. "That bathroom is entirely too small! How are two people supposed to share it? This is a school, not prison!"

Belle chuckles. "You should be really grateful for that bathroom. The alternative is the shared bathrooms in Stratford Hall."

My eyebrows rise. "The what now?"

She points to the window, where a large and imposing building is just across a small pathway. "That's the student dorms. Each floor has a different grade, and the boys and girls are separated out on different hallways. They all share a common bathroom on each floor."

My eyes go wide. "What kind of torture is that?"

She shrugs. "It's a boarding school."

"So why do we have a bathroom if no one else does?" I already know the obvious answer – money – but it doesn't make sense because Belle's mom doesn't have much of that.

Belle tugs at her sleeve again, a nervous habit. "These are the staff dorms. The staff has private bathrooms. I got moved here a few years ago."

"Ew... this is a staff building? I don't want to live next to teachers."

"It's mostly staff, not teachers. Like office workers, and TA's and stuff. And honestly, not many people live here. I think most of the rooms are empty."

I roll my eyes. I guess the benefits of a private bathroom, no matter how small, outweigh being in a building that won't have fun parties.

"There was a memo for you," Belle says, turning to the bulletin board that's hanging on her side of the dorm room. She plucks off an envelope and hands it to me.

It's a typed letter from the dean, welcoming me to Shelfbrooke Academy. He's included my schedule and told me to find Ms. Beverly in the front office as soon as I arrive.

"Do you think they'll make me start classes today?" I ask.

"I don't know." Belle sits on her bed and looks out the window.

"Are you on lunch break or something?" I ask.

"Not really," she says, messing with her sleeve again.

"Well... are you going to show me where the front office is?"

Belle's nervous expression comes back. My cousin is extremely weird. She takes a deep breath. "I'm really busy, but I can tell you where to go."

I lift a curious eyebrow. She doesn't look busy. She tells me the way to the front desk, and she also warns me that I should put on a uniform. Uh, no thanks.

"Uniforms are mandatory," she says, biting her bottom lip. "You have to wear them at all times."

I put a hand on my hip. "You're not wearing one."

Her cheeks flush red. Something tells me I shouldn't have mentioned that, but I don't know why. She's a student here too, after all.

"I'll wait until I go to classes to wear that stupid thing," I say, casting a scornful glance at the pile of uniforms on my bed. "And thanks for letting me borrow your sheets. I'll order my own online and have them shipped overnight to me."

Belle's directions were easy enough and soon I'm entering the main building where the front desk is. Everything about this place screams prestigious and expensive, and it makes me wonder why they put us away in tiny little dorm rooms. Shouldn't students get to live in luxury when their parents are paying a ton of money for their education?

The woman behind the front counter has bright blonde hair pulled into a neat bun on top of her head. Her face is round and friendly.

"Hi, dear," she says, beaming at me.

"Are you Ms. Beverly?"

"I am. Most people call me Ms. Bev," she says with a smile. "What can I do for you?"

"I'm new," I say, holding out the schedule I'd received in my letter from the dean. "I was told to come talk to you."

"Oh, perfect! Hello there, Miss Brass." Ms. Bev stands up and shakes my hand. "It's so lovely to meet you. We don't usually have new students in the middle of the school year."

"Yeah it was... a surprise," I say.

She picks up her desk phone. "I have a student who will show you around campus. Give me just a moment. You can wait right over there."

I thank her and go stand in the lobby while I wait to meet the first student at Shelfbrooke who isn't related to me. My phone rings from my back pocket, and although I wish it was Henry calling to tell me he misses me and wants only me, not Viv, and that he will wait until I graduate and move back, it's not him. It's my mother.

"Hello," I say, in the most apathetic voice I can make.

"Did you make it there safely?"

"Yep," I say, heaving a sigh.

"Great. I got a notice from the shipping company and your luggage will be delivered in a few hours. They'll probably call you to the office or something."

"Wonderful," I say in a way that shows I clearly don't think it's wonderful at all.

Mom sighs. "Sophia, why are you being like this?"

"Oh I don't know," I say. "Maybe because you forced me to go to some stupid school for no reason at all. It sucks here, Mom. The rooms are small and everything is old and ancient, and the uniforms are the most hideous thing I've ever seen—"

"Sophia!" Mom snaps. "I will not have you talking to me this way. You are too old to be such a brat."

I grit my teeth. I hate that word. Brat. I hate it more than the other B word which most people find more offensive. Nope. This word is so much worse to me. I've been called it my whole life. It's not my fault I am the way I am.

I hold the phone close to my ear and I regret the words the second I think of them, but that doesn't stop me from saying it. "I'm clearly not too old to be a brat, mother, because you're the biggest brat I know, and you're twice my age."

"Sophia-" Mom starts, but I'm done listening. She's already stuck me in this crappy school in the cold New England weather with my weird cousin. I hang up the phone.

When I turn around, a gorgeous guy is standing there, blue eyes wide as he watches me. I close my eyes for a brief moment. Of course. *Of course* some hot guy was here and heard that whole conversation.

I hold my head high and start to walk away.

"Sophia?" he says, stepping over to block my exit. "I'm Declan. I'm here to show you around campus."

CHAPTER FIVE

MY DEFENSES SHOOT UP. My metaphorical walls that protect me from all the rich bullies in my life rise up and protect me. It's instant. It's instinctual. Instead of allowing myself to feel embarrassed because this random guy just heard me whining and complaining to my mom, I put on a brave face. I hold my head up, my shoulders back. This guy—what was his name? Declan—is taller than I am. But I have perfected the art of looking down on someone. You must treat everyone as if they have no power over you. No ability to make you hurt. No way to make you feel embarrassed.

You are better than they are. That's the only way to feel as though you won't break apart.

I draw in a deep breath and look him over. He's not wearing the Shelfbrooke uniform, but rather a dark blue jumpsuit with the Shelfbrooke logo stitched on the chest.

"What are you?" I say, letting the tone of my voice convey that I'm better than him. "Some kind of janitor? They sent a janitor to show me around?"

"I'm a gardener," he says. "I'm also a student."

I flip my hair over my shoulder. "Why?"

He looks confused for a second, and then shrugs. "Because some people need jobs to pay their bills."

I roll my eyes, then hold out my hand and wave for him to get started. "I don't want to keep you from your job, so let's get on with this."

He turns and opens a door that leads outside, holding it open as I walk through. I know I should thank him because that's what decent humans do, but I'm still horribly embarrassed from that phone call with my mother. Normally I wouldn't think twice about this kind of thing, but as I walk on by without thanking him, I feel bad about it. Maybe because he's a normie, like Viv would say. He's not some trust fund jerk that hangs in the wealthy circles in California. He's just a regular guy. He even has a job at the school. How lame is that?

"Is this your first time a Shelfbrooke?" he asks.

"Yep."

"What grade are you in?"

"I'm a senior."

He stops walking for half a second and looks at me, brows curiously pulled together before he keeps walking. "Okay. I'm a senior, too."

"I know it's weird," I say with a sigh. "It's my parents... they decided to send me here for no reason because it's only a few months until graduation."

"Where did you go before?"

"I was homeschooled. Private tutor."

"Cool."

"Yeah, it was cool," I say, clenching my jaw as I remember the good old days, aka-last week. "My parents are the worst."

"So let me tell you about Shelfbrooke," Declan says, putting on a cheery smile that doesn't reach his eyes. "We're co-ed, and we have a long history of being rugby and lacrosse champions. Our mascot is the Black Knights."

"Sports are boring," I say. Mainly because I don't have anything else to say and I'm still so fuming mad about my mom that I can't think straight. I just want to pick a fight. I want to tear someone down.

"Right, well, we have other things too. There's five hundred acres and many of them are gardens. Shelfbrooke is famous for them."

I roll my eyes. "Boring."

He takes a deep breath and tries again. "So over

there is Kellylynch Hall. That's where your classes will be. If you have your schedule on you, I can show you where all your classes are."

"I'm not an idiot," I say. "I'll figure it out tomorrow."

"Right," he says. "So the dining hall is over there, and they have pretty good food. Dinner starts around six p.m. Oh, and phones are allowed. That's a fairly new rule."

"Thank God," I say, touching my pocket where my phone is. "I don't think I could survive without it."

"Most people can't. Also, they're addicted to Knight Watch."

"Knight Watch?"

"It's the school's own social media app."

I roll my eyes. "Lame."

I can tell my constant complaints are bugging him, and I kind of like it. It's almost fun to say something sarcastic after everything he tells me. Deep down I know I must be a terrible person, but I'm so angry any my parents for making me go here that I just don't care right now.

Declan shows me around more of the school and tells me about their stupid rules. Curfew is at nine on weekdays and ten on weekends. Um, what? That's so lame.

"Don't worry," he says, shoving his hands into the

pockets of his jumpsuit. "The popular kids tend to disregard the curfew and get away with it."

I grin. "You think I'm popular?"

His hair falls in his eyes and he shakes it away as he looks at me. "You're exactly the type of girl who gets popular at a place like this."

My lips press together as I look him over. "I like you, Declan the janitor."

"Gardener," he corrects.

I roll my eyes. "Same thing."

Declan nods. "Yep," he says, exhaling a sarcastic sigh. "They are exactly the same thing."

He stops at the large building in front of us. "This is Stratford Hall. It's the student dorms. Each grade has its own floor, so you'll be up on the fourth floor. I can take you there now if you know your room number."

"No, I'm actually staying in the staff dorms," I say. He gives me another look, like he just can't quite figure me out.

"I'm sharing a room with my cousin," I explain. That doesn't take away any of his confusion.

"I'll show you Stratford Hall anyway, because there's also the student common area so you'll probably spend a lot of time in here. The ground level is the common area. There are study rooms, and couches and televisions and stuff. It's where we spend our time when we're sick of our roommates."

"Roommates?" I say. "You have more than one?"

"There's three of us in our dorm."

I make a gagging sound. "Oh my God, I would drop out if I had to share a tiny room with two other people."

He doesn't say anything. He just holds open the door to Stratford Hall. Inside, I see the common areas in all their glory, and I am not a fan. There aren't too many students in here, but they all look at me like I'm something they scraped off the bottom of their shoe. What the crap is that? I'm Sophia Brass.

"These people could show some respect," I say after the tour of the dorm building is over.

"What do you mean by that?" Declan asks.

I shrug. "Everyone was looking at me."

"You're the new girl. They're going to look."

I shake my head. "No. Not like that. They were looking at me like—like..."

"Like you think you're too good to be here?"

My jaw flies open. "Um, rude."

He shrugs. "That's the vibe you're giving off."

"Well maybe I am too good to be here," I snap. "This school is stupid. Tiny dorms and ugly uniforms, and they make you work a job here like some kind of loser."

Declan's jaw stiffens.

"No, I'm not insulting you," I say, trying to backpedal. "I'm just..."

"Insulting me," he says, finishing my sentence for me. "I actually don't think I'm a loser for working here. I like it. I want to work here. It's a privilege to tend to these famous gardens."

I roll my eyes. "No one wants to work."

He snorts out a laugh. "Is this your first time leaving whatever ivory tower you were born in and joining the real world?"

I can't believe he just snapped at me like that. Most people don't have the nerve. I stare into his deep blue eyes, my jaw set. My body ready to pick a fight and tear him down. I can make fun of him for being poor a thousand times over. But I have nothing else to say to insult him. He's gorgeous. I can't poke fun at his height or his ears or anything. Declan is absolutely perfect. And that makes me dislike him even more. Gorgeous guys throw themselves at me. And the ones who don't, can't be trusted. Declan is definitely not throwing himself at me right now.

I decide to ignore his commentary. I don't want to get caught asking stupid questions on my first day of school tomorrow, so I figure I should learn all I can from him now. I point to an older building that's off in the distance. "What's that?"

He peers in the direction I'm pointing. "That's Kingsbere Hall. It's mostly abandoned... you won't have classes there."

"Mostly abandoned?"

He shrugs. "The rich kids have secret parties in the basement."

"Cool," I say.

"You'd have to be invited."

I fold my arms across my chest. "Of course I'll be invited."

Two girls in Shelfbrooke uniforms walk by. They look like freshman, or maybe sophomores. "Hi Declan," they both say at the same time.

"Hey," he says, giving them a friendly wave.

The girls giggle and wave, picking up their pace as they walk by. I can't say I blame them. I would totally crush on Declan if I was fourteen. But now I'm almost eighteen and I know way better than that.

"So, is the tour over?" I ask.

His tongue slips over his bottom lip as he thinks, his gaze sweeping across the campus. "I think so. Do you have any other questions?"

I shake my head. "Lame school, stupid rules. There's not much else I need to know."

CHAPTER SIX

BEFORE I GO BACK to my dorm, I wander around the back of the building and to a little courtyard that's lush and green despite the cold weather. There's a concrete fountain in the middle with water sprinkling out of it. I glance around to make sure I'm alone and then I call Viv. It feels so surreal being here, and it's only been a few hours, and I have no idea how I'll survive. I may not like her that much, but I need Viv. I need a familiar face to tell me it'll be okay.

The phone rings and rings. She doesn't answer.

I hang up when her voicemail picks up because I'm pretty sure I might start crying if I try to leave a message. I really, really, really don't want to be here. A few minutes pass, with me standing near the fountain trying to look normal, but Viv never calls me back.

Finally, I give up and walk back to the staff dorms. I didn't truly explore that building the last time I was there. I just know it's long and narrow, with one main hallway and rooms on one side. Maybe there's also a common room, or a teacher's lounge or something. But I guess they wouldn't let me hang out since I'm a student.

Reluctantly, I walk back inside and to dorm room number 62. The door is locked when I turn the handle. I tap on it. "Belle? It's me."

She opens the door, her round eyes looking all around me.

"I'm alone," I say.

"Good."

She locks the door back.

"Is there a reason you keep the door locked all the time?"

"Obviously there's a reason," she says, padding across the tile floor in her plaid house shoes. "It's to keep us safe."

"Is the school a dangerous place?"

She gives a noncommittal wobble of her head as she drops onto her bed, her focus shifting to her open laptop.

Whatever. I begin hanging up the uniforms in my closet, and I make my bed with the sheets Belle lends me. She gives me one of her many pillows, and I thank her, and then I sit on my mattress and open up my laptop. I order all new bedding and use my credit card to have it shipped here as fast as possible.

There's a loud knock at the door and my cousin jumps, her laptop skittering across the bed. "Who is it?" she whispers. "Did you invite someone?"

She's somehow managed to turn a shade paler than usual, which I didn't think was possible. The girl's skin looks like she's never been outside. Her eyes are wide and I can practically hear her heart pounding in the silence that follows.

"I'm sure it's nothing," I say, getting up and walking over to the door.

"Wait!" she whisper-yells. "Use the peephole."

Frowning, I push back a dark scarf that's been thumbtacked to the door, revealing a peephole hidden underneath it. "Yay!" I say, stepping back and throwing open the door.

My luggage is there. Along with a guy in a UPS uniform. "Sign here," he says, handing me a tablet. I scribble my name and thank him.

"Lock the door," Belle says as I bring my luggage inside. I do as she asks, and I really, really want to tell her she's being overly paranoid, but I keep my thoughts to myself. It was one thing to be rude to that gardener guy earlier. This is my cousin and I have to live with her.

The next couple of hours pass easily while I unpack

my stuff and find a new home for it all on my half of the dorm room. Belle watches me silently, her attention shifting from her computer to me every few minutes.

"Um, Sophia?" she says after I've arranged my makeup on top of the dresser. There is no room for a vanity mirror here, so this is my best place to put it.

"Yeah?" I say, uncapping some lip gloss since this chilly January weather is making my lips dry.

"Could you maybe tell me when you're expecting a delivery, or a visitor or something? If I know ahead of time, then I won't get so freaked out."

"Okay, sure," I say, sliding the lip gloss applicator over my bottom lip. "My new sheets are getting delivered tomorrow, but it'll probably arrive when you're in class so it won't be a big deal."

"No, I'll be here," she says, looking back at her computer screen.

"Why? Are you sick or just playing hooky?"

She chews on the inside of her lip. "My mom didn't tell you?"

"Tell me what?"

"Anything about me?"

I think back to my very brief encounter with Aunt Kate. "Nope."

"Hmm," she says. "Well... I do alternative school. It's online. My teachers visit with me once every few weeks to check on my progress, and I just listen to the lectures with a webcam."

"Why on earth would you do that? This room is depressing. Don't you want to go to your classes and socialize?"

Her eyes widen for a second and then she shakes her head, looking all small and scared again. "I like online learning. It's… it's better for me."

I can tell there is more to this story. Some hidden reason my cousin is the why she is, but I can also tell that she does not want to talk about it.

I sit on my bed and look at my printed class schedule. "I guess this means you won't be able to walk with me to class tomorrow?"

She frowns and looks down at her hands. "No, sorry."

I don't want my disappointment to show through, so I shrug and shake off all my first-day-of-school jitters. "Eh, who cares. I'll be fine. Once people realize they have East Coast Royalty here, they'll all be begging to be my friend."

I WALK with purpose the next morning, even though my uniform is annoying, and I'm only vaguely sure where I'm supposed to go. The fabric is crisp from being dry cleaned, and the skirt feels annoying on my skin. It's too stuffy, too prep school. I'm more of a laid-back fashionista myself. I'm not into all these buttons and creases.

The campus is filled with students as I make my way to Kellylynch Hall for my first class of the day. It's English, which should be simple enough. I try to spot a group of popular students so I can make my new set of friends, but it's hard to tell everyone apart when they're wearing the same clothes. Some people try to set themselves apart, though. I see Airpods in ears, and luxury brand black shoes. Diamond bracelets and gorgeous real hair extensions.

But all of these things just separate out the wealthier students from the others. They don't tell me who is popular.

I guess it doesn't totally matter, I tell myself as I walk with a little more pep in my step. Once people realize that Sophia Brass is here, I'll become the most popular student. So who cares who is currently popular? I'm about to take over here.

Honestly, I'm a little surprised that no one has said anything to me by the time I get to the English hallway. It's all the way up on the third floor, and I'm in such a hurry to get there before the bell rings, I don't really stop to admire the intricate architecture of the old building. I don't really care if I'm late and make some kind of grand entrance in front of everyone—in fact, I kind of prefer that—but I do remember reading over the strict rules of the school and getting a tardy is not a good idea. The last thing I need is any kind of disciplinary record to make my parents show their wrath in an even worse way.

English Lit with Professor Harding is at the very end of the hallway. I find the classroom easily enough and slip inside. All eyes are immediately on me. I uphold my confidence and walk straight to the teacher's desk where a middle-aged man with a slender build sits, looking through some papers.

"Hello," I say, "I'm Sophia Brass."

Professor Harding gazes up at me, and he couldn't look any more bored if he tried. "Good for you. Have a seat."

"I'm a new student."

"*Obviously*," he says, his eyes meeting mine for a fraction of a second before looking away. "In this classroom, we don't waste our time reciting clear facts, Ms. Brass. Please take your seat."

Someone snickers. Not laughs, not chuckles, but *snickers*. A snide, rude sound that's totally making fun of me. And then everyone else does the same.

I refuse to acknowledge any of these people. And I definitely won't let them know that they're bothering me. I scan the room, find an empty desk in the back, and sit down.

I had the good sense to bring my laptop as well as pack a binder with paper and pens, and I'm glad I did.

That gardener guy didn't bother telling me that everyone here uses a laptop during class to take their notes, but I've seen enough television to have guessed that was a possibility.

I open my laptop, ignore the stares from people, and try to focus on the days' lecture.

Only... I already know all of this stuff.

The same thing happens in second period. I take a seat without talking to the teacher, who doesn't care or notice that I'm here, and then the lesson begins and they're learning stuff I already know.

The students are not nice. No one says hello. No one asks for my name.

I eat lunch with Belle in our dorm. She doesn't ask me why, and I don't bother telling her.

The rest of my classes are all equally awful. The lessons are boring because I already know it all, and the students ignore me.

During my last class of the day, I'm considering that maybe I should introduce myself to these people so that I can finally make some friends, but I can never seem to pluck up the courage to do it. This isn't like back at home, where everyone knew me and everyone wanted to be my friend. I've never had to make first contact with someone. People just come to me.

These Shelfbrooke kids obviously have no idea who I am, but how do I tell them? I can't exactly stand up in the middle of the classroom and announce: "By the way, I'm Sophia Brass, of the Brass fortune, yes that Sophia, the one with almost a million followers on Instagram. Now that you know who I am, you can all start begging to be my friend."

I snort at the thought as I imagine that scene playing out in my head. I would never actually do that, but it would be funny. And it might actually get results. But still – I am *not* that desperate.

"Excuse me," my fourth period chemistry teacher says. "Sophia Brass, is it?"

I jolt, looking up at her. "Yes?"

"Is there something funny about these molecules?"

Everyone turns to look at me.

"No."

"Then please refrain from laughing in my class."

Oops.

A few people throw sarcastic looks my way, but this is actually a good thing. The teacher just said my name in front of everyone. Now maybe, finally, these idiots will want to be my friend now that they know who I am.

The teacher—I forget her name—finishes up her lecture and then looks out at the class. "Time to pair up with a partner. You know the rules. New semester, new partner. You can't stick with your same buddy from last time."

I sit up in my desk. Perfect.

Only... it's not perfect. I expect everyone to get up and walk over to me and ask to be my partner, now that they know who I am.

But no one does.

Some people just get up and shuffle their chairs to the person next to them. No one really makes a big deal about it, but one thing is very, very clear. No one is asking me to be their partner.

A few minutes go by and I sit here, frozen in place, unwilling to get up and ask someone to take pity on me. And that's exactly what it would be... pity.

Maybe the east coast is a lot different than I imagined. Maybe these people have no idea who I am because they're stuck in this stuffy boarding school. For all I know, the school blocks Instagram or something.

Very well then. I swallow back the awkward and horrible feeling of being left out and I look at my laptop and pretend everything is okay. I'll just be my own partner. That's how it works when you're homeschooled, after all. I'm good at working alone.

"Everyone pair up!" the teacher says. "No one works solo."

I cringe. She's talking about me. She has to be. I'm too embarrassed to look around the room and see who isn't paired up yet. That would only draw attention to me, the epic loser, the new girl with no partner.

A shadow falls over my laptop screen. I look up and see the gardener Declan standing there, an old laptop tucked under his arm. "Hi, partner," he says, dropping down into the empty seat next to me.

"You don't have to be my partner just because you feel sorry for me."

His beautiful blue eyes look over mine and my heartbeat seems too slow. It thumps three times as Declan watches me. *Say you don't feel sorry for me*, I think. And then Declan says, "Yes I do."

CHAPTER SEVEN

I SHOVE my key into the lock of my dorm room and twist, hard. The rusty old lock doesn't wiggle much, and I glance up at the gold numbers on the door, scared that I'm trying to get into the wrong dorm.

But it's the right number—my key just sucks. I twist and wiggle it again, and it finally turns a quarter turn, but not enough to open the lock.

The click of the deadbolt twisting comes from the other side. Belle opens the door.

"My stupid key doesn't work," I say, huffing into the room and throwing my bag on my bed, not even caring that my laptop is in there. I'll just buy a new one if it breaks.

"It's the lock," she says, quickly closing the door

again. "It's old and doesn't get used much, so the key doesn't work well."

"That's crap," I say, glaring at the offending door. "We'll call maintenance and have them fix it."

"No, that's fine. It's fine." Belle's smile says there's something more to her thoughts, but she goes back to her bed and her laptop. I swear that's all she ever does is sit on her bed, doing school work or whatever.

"Today sucked," I say, plopping onto my bed. "It really, really sucked."

"Why?" Belle glances up from her laptop screen. "The work is hard, but you get used to it."

"No, the work is actually easy. My tutors taught me this stuff a long time ago. It's everything else that's hard."

I want to keep talking, but I stop, because saying anything more would be admitting a weakness. Showing that I'm not the strong girl I pretend to be. But Belle is all ears now.

"What happened?" she says, leaning forward in anticipation of hearing the story.

I roll my eyes. I don't want to tell her, but she's family. I hold up a finger and give her a threatening glare. "If I tell you, you don't say a word to anyone."

"Promise," she says.

I fall back on my bed, staring up at our vaulted dorm room ceiling. "I don't even know where to begin.

Everyone is rude. Or they just ignore me. I don't know what's worse. The teachers aren't too nice either. And then I got stuck with a pity lab partner."

"A what?" Belle says. I see her from the corner of my eye, sitting rail straight, absolutely captivated by everything I'm saying. Her long dark hair is twisted into twin braids that fall down her shoulders, but they're all fuzzy and slept on. She needs to rebraid them before she goes anywhere.

"A pity lab partner," I repeat. "It was awful. He only agreed to partner up with me because no one else wanted to."

"Declan's nice like that," Belle says.

I sit up, the hairs on the back of my neck prickling. "How do you know it was Declan?"

"Knight Watch."

She rotates her laptop screen and I see what looks like a social media feed, refreshing every few seconds. "What is that?" I say, although I realize what it is a few seconds later. Declan told me about Knight Watch on our tour yesterday.

"They post people's chem partners on there?"

Belle shrugs. "Someone mentioned that you were in class and had partnered with Declan."

"How was it posted?" I ask, eyeing her computer screen even though it's too far away to see from where

I'm sitting. "Was it like, 'Sophia Brass is here, Declan is so lucky to be her friend'?"

Belle's expression tells me the answer before she speaks. "Not really."

I roll my eyes and fall back on my bed. "I hate this school. I hate the people. I hate the classes. And I hate these stupid uniforms."

I close my eyes and take a deep breath. I try to imagine I'm lying in my bed at home—or better yet, on a yoga mat at our country club back in Malibu. *I'm taking a calming yoga class, I'm back home. I'm where I belong. Everyone adores me. I am totally happy...*

"I wish I could tell you it's not so bad, but...I can't." Belle's voice pulls me from my daydream, but it's just as well because I can't actually relax right now. My brain is too smart. It knows full well that we aren't in a yoga studio in Malibu.

I open my eyes. "Is this why you do your schoolwork online?"

She gets all fidgety, biting her bottom lip and examining her fingernails. That kind of gives her away, but eventually she says, "Yes."

"What happened?" I sit up and walk over to her side of the room for the first time. It feels a little weird, like I'm getting in her personal space or something, but she is my cousin after all. We were friends as kids. And she looks like she's hurting right now.

I sit at the foot of her bed. "Did someone hurt you?"

She swallows, still looking at her hands. "No."

"You can talk to me."

Her brown eyes look up at mine. She looks so fragile, and so sad, and it makes my heart hurt. Then, I get angry. "Who made you this way? Was it a guy? One of those bratty girls? I'll put them in their place—"

"No, Sophia. It was no one. It was me. I'm the problem."

I release the breath I'd held in, disappointed that I can't direct my anger onto someone who hurt my cousin. "It was you? What does that even mean?"

She nods. Swallows again.

"It was freshman year. I was... I was walking to class and..." Her chest rises with a deep breath. She pulls her straggly braids over one shoulder and then tosses them back again. Her eyes meet mine, and then she looks away.

I can tell this is hard for her to talk about, but holy crap I am intrigued. I want to scream *just tell me already!* But I hold back. I wait for what feels like an eternity, and then she clears her throat.

"I don't know what happened. My body freaked out.

My brain freaked out. I couldn't breathe. I couldn't see. I felt like I was dying. Like, literally, seriously, dying."

She says it all really fast, like it's the only way she can get it out. "I fell to the ground. My vision was blurring and coming in and out of focus. My chest hurt. I swear my heart was going to explode. Someone called an ambulance, and after all these tests and stuff, they just said I had a panic attack."

She scoffs, her upper lip curling in disgust. "They said it was nothing, and that I was fine and I should get over it. So I went back to class—well, I tried to—but every time I step outside, the panic attack would come back."

"Wow."

She nods. "I don't understand what's wrong with me. Doctors are no help. It was the start of my freshman year, so I didn't really have many friends, and the girls I did hang out with just quit talking to me. My old roommate complained that I was annoying her because I spent like three weeks crying and panicking about the idea of having another panic attack in our room. They ended up moving me to the staff dorms so I could be alone. And this is where I've been ever since."

My eyes widen. "You haven't left this dorm in three years?"

I swear, if my cousin gnaws on her bottom lip for

much longer, it's going to fall right off. She nods. "Not really. I've been to the doctor a few times, but... I just stay. My panic attacks stopped once I quit leaving. I feel safe here."

"You haven't left in three years," I repeat, more to myself than to her. "This isn't normal."

"I know," she says with a snort. "Trust me, I know. I hate it, but I also don't mind it. I get to stay here where it's safe and I feel fine."

Suddenly the stuck door lock makes sense. It's gotten all rusted over from the outside since it's never used.

"No, it's not okay." I stand up and reach for her hand. "I'm going to help you. Let's go outside."

"No!" She shrinks back, pulling her hands close to her body. "I'm not leaving. Don't even joke about that."

"You have to leave sometime," I say, glancing toward the door. "You will graduate this year and then what? They won't let you live here forever."

She shrugs. "Maybe they will. Dean Thomas is really nice."

"They won't," I say.

"The staff dorms are mostly empty. They'll probably forget that I'm even here. I could stay for decades."

"You cannot be that delusional," I say.

Her nostrils flare, and I know I've struck a chord. I probably shouldn't have called her that.

Belle turns to her computer, focusing her attention on that instead of me. "I'm not talking about it anymore. You wanted the truth, and I told you the truth. Now let it go."

"Fine."

I go back to my side of the bed, leaving behind the scent of cinnamon and coffee from the candle on her nightstand. I might let it go for now, but I'm not letting it go forever. It's kind of screwed up that my Aunt Kate just allows this. Belle needs help. A good therapist or something. She can't just live at Shelfbrooke Academy forever.

"We can talk about you, if you want," Belle says softly after enough time has passed that we've both settled down. "I don't want to make you mad, I just really can't talk about myself, okay?"

"Fine, let's talk about me."

I yank off my school uniform and toss it into my clothing hamper. "How do you know Declan?"

"Everyone knows him. He's really nice. His family has worked here for like, ever."

"As gardeners?" I say.

She nods.

"That's probably how he can afford the tuition. I guess it's like, kids of the employees get in free or something."

"So why was he your pity partner?" she asks.

I really want to forget the whole day, but she just told me something majorly personal, so I return the favor. I tell her about my craptastic first day of school, and how he came over and saved me from not having a partner.

"How was it?" she says, wiggling her eyebrows. "Spending all class period with him?"

I shrug. "We barely talked. It was mostly just taking notes. I don't know why we had to partner up. I think the teacher is just evil."

My stomach twists and I hope it doesn't show on my face. How deep down, I wanted to be friendly with Declan, but it felt impossible. I'd been rude to him when we first met, and he'd been rightfully cold to me. How do you become friends after something like that? Plus, I think my heart knows that it's better to stay away. That boy is cuter than he has any right to be, and I do not need to go getting a crush on some lowly gardener. I have a senator's son back at home. And yeah, Henry isn't exactly waiting on me, but that doesn't mean I can't win him back from Viv once I finally get graduate this stupid place and go home.

"I just thought my first day would be better than this," I say, feeling a blush creep into my cheeks. "I thought I would make friends."

"There's a party tonight in Kingsbere Hall," Belle says, perking up. "You could go. Maybe you'll make some friends there?"

"Will you come with me?"

She gives me a look, and I grin. "It was worth trying."

"No, it wasn't," she says, rolling her eyes.

"What kind of party is it?" I'm no stranger to parties, but something tells me a boarding school shindig won't be nearly as much fun as the ones I go to back at home.

"Just one of the parties the senior class throws. It's held in the basement. I get invited to all of them, but I've never been. Everyone says good things about the parties on Knight Watch though. So it's probably fun."

I consider it for a moment. "I'm guessing they don't wear uniforms to these secret parties?"

"It's safe to say they do not."

I grin, thinking of my gorgeous black dress hanging in the closet. My first day at Shelfbrooke totally sucked, but I'm not a quitter.

I'm Sophia Brass.

And I'm about to show these New England losers how a Cali girl parties.

CHAPTER EIGHT

KINGSBERE HALL HAS to be the oldest building on campus. It's way off the normal pathways and looks abandoned. Ivy walls cover the red bricks, creeping up and over the windows as if nature is trying to take back the old building. Or hide something from getting out. I smile to myself, thinking of all the haunted stories you could invent about an old building like this.

It's a chilly night, and my black pantyhose aren't doing a single thing to keep me warm. But at least I look totally hot in my black dress, ruby red ballet flats, and long silver teardrop necklace. This is a much better look than those dumb uniforms.

The air is sweet, scented by the nearby gardens and the tall hedge wall that lines the cobblestone walkway as I make my way toward Kingsbere Hall. It's dark out since it's just past ten o'clock at night, and the dusty glow of the few lampposts that dot the sidewalks barely provide any light this far away from the main campus.

The shadows make the gardens feel slightly creepy, despite their beautiful appearance in the daytime. The closer I get to the building, the more I start to feel weird.

No, I tell myself as the fluttery, awful feeling stirs in my stomach. I am *not* nervous. Why would I be nervous? Parties are my thing. They're what I'm good at.

But *nervous* is exactly what I feel like.

There's a soft thumping of music sounding from the building, where the seniors-only party rages down in the basement. I'm just a few steps way now, so close to the door that I could reach out and touch it. But something stops me. Intuition, maybe.

I hear laughter in the distance, and I jump, rushing off to the side where an overgrown bush blocks me from view.

Why am I hiding? What is wrong with me?

Still, I stand here in the chilly air, hidden in the shadows while two girls talk excitedly to each other as they approach the building. I should step out, say hello, introduce myself. But again, that weird intuition feeling something stops me.

"Yo, wait up!" a guy calls from way down the side-walk. I peer at him through the leaves, and see that it's actually two guys walking together, their bodies illuminating under the lamppost and then disappearing again when the sidewalk gets dark. The girls stop and wait for them to catch up.

"There better be some hot girls at this party," the guy says, popping his collar and running a hand over the top of his hair. "I'm ready to get out there and date again."

"I heard some new girl just enrolled," his friend says. "Apparently she's pretty cute."

I grin.

"Nah, man, stay away from that girl," the first guy says.

My grin disappears.

"Yeah, it's some rich California brat," the of the girls says. "Chad told us she's not worth the effort."

There's that stupid B word again. And who on earth is this Chad guy deciding to judge me for no reason? I see red. I want to walk out and give them a piece of my mind, but I don't.

"You can tell she thinks she's better than everyone, and I'm like, *really*? Your parents are corrupt hedge fund managers. Ugh."

"People like that make me sick."

"Everyone on Knight Watch has made a pact to ignore the stuck-up princess."

I don't know who is saying what now, and I'm too

scared to peek out from the bushes in case they see me. My heart aches. My pulse races in my ears. I can't believe the things I'm hearing.

"Why did she have to be hot?" A guy says. "People like that should be ugly. It's only fair."

A girl snorts. "I don't think she's that pretty. She's pathetic."

The music gets louder as the doors open, and then everything goes quiet again. I don't step out of the shadows. I don't want to risk seeing anyone else on the sidewalk, so I turn the opposite direction and slip into the gardens. It's like a labyrinth in here, but at least there are plenty of places to hide if I hear anyone else.

My cheeks are cold and wet, and it takes a second to realize I'm crying. I don't even know when the tears started, but now that I'm aware of it, I can't stop. I can't believe I'm crying. I don't cry. I am strong. And important. And loved back home. At least... that's what I tell myself. Do the people at home really love me? Or am I just some rich connection they use to get into parties and go on free vacations?

I tuck into a little alcove in the gardens, one so dark I can barely see the white concrete bench as I sit down on it, covering my face with my hands as I let out more sobs.

How did I go from popular, lovable, and cool in one day to pathetic outcast in the next? And why are they hating on my parents? I mean, my parents aren't exactly the best people ever, and I don't know what exactly hedge funds are, but they aren't me. I shouldn't be hated because someone hates what my parents do for a living. They shouldn't publish me without even meeting me just because of my family.

I don't know how much time passes while I sit on this bench feeling sorry for myself, but I do know that I am freezing cold, and absolutely sick of crying. I don't know how my life went from perfect to miserable so fast.

I take out my phone and stare at my home screen. Viv hasn't texted me at all. No one else has, either. I check my social media. All my friends are posting about their epic parties and perfect lives, and no one seems to miss me. It only makes me want to cry again, so I shove the stupid phone back in my clutch.

I look up at the sky, which is dark and dotted with sparkling stars.

Maybe Belle has it all figured out. Maybe it is easier to sit in our dorm room all day. I get up, wipe my cheeks, and start walking back to the staff dorms.

Only... it's not so easy because it's dark out here in the gardens. I think I came from this way, but as I turn around a corner, I feel completely lost. So, I turn back and retrace my steps. Then I go the opposite way. Large shrubs form walls that are just about as tall as I am, and the paths that are beautiful in the day become scary at night. I meander through some shadowy pathways trying not to freak out.

Finally, I turn and recognize a concrete statue of a little girl. I saw that statue when I entered the gardens, so I must be close to the way out of here.

I make a sharp turn and smack straight into a tall boy that smells amazing. Like freshly laundered clothes and summer days and—*oh crap*.

"You," I say, taking a step backward.

The moonlight glints off his necklace, and the intricate silver pendant catches my attention for a moment. It looks like some kind of Celtic circle or something.

"Lost?" Declan says, a bit of amusement in his voice.

"No," I say.

He folds his arms over his chest. He's handsome in his school uniform, but right now he's wearing dark jeans and a black T-shirt and he looks even better than usual. I grit my teeth and shove out the thought.

"Sure you're not lost?"

"I know exactly where I am," I snap.

"Is that why you've walked this path three times in the last ten minutes?"

My cheeks flush. "Seriously?"

He chuckles. "I'll show you the way out."

I want to refuse his help, but I'm also cold and miserable and just want to go home.

"How come you didn't announce yourself the first time I walked by?" I ask as he leads the way out of this labyrinth. "Or were you being a creepy stalker who enjoys watching me get lost?"

I really hope he didn't see me cry. I'm pretty sure I was alone in that alcove when the real waterworks came flowing out of me, but maybe I wasn't. As if I needed to be any more humiliated tonight, let's add a hot boy seeing me cry like a loser.

"I come here to get some peace and quiet," he says, ignoring my stalker comment. "Your annoying pacing back and forth ruined that."

"You sit in the gardens in the middle of the night all by yourself?" I ask.

He holds up his phone, which has a pair of headphones wrapped around it. "I come out here and watch my favorite TV shows. It's the only way to get away from my loud, obnoxious roommates."

"Makes sense," I say, shivering as a blast of cold air rips right through me.

"You're not dressed for the outdoors," he says, turning left in a place I didn't realize could turn left. But sure enough, there's a path between the shadowy hedges that are taller than we are.

"I was going to a party, but I decided not to."

"Hmm," is all he says.

We walk in silence for a few more minutes, and then he turns, and we're out of the gardens. "Your dorm is that way," he says, pointing toward the staff dorms.

"Thank you." There's a shiver in my voice because it's gotten colder now that we're out of the gardens.

Declan looks like wants to say something, but he doesn't. We're standing under a lamppost, and once again I see his necklace. "That's pretty," I say, pointing to the silver pendant. It's circular, with some kind of design on it that looks meticulously carved.

"It was my grandfather's," he says, wrapping his hand around the pendant.

"Well... it's cool."

He nods once. I take that as my cue to leave. Clearly, he was just being nice by escorting me out of the gardens. Just like he was being nice in chemistry class. He probably didn't even care that I made it out safely, he just wanted a place to watch his show without having me wandering around lost and annoying him. I turn and walk away, and with each step farther away, I'm secretly hoping he'll call out my name and offer to hang out with me.

But he doesn't. Declan is not my friend.

I'm not sure anyone is.

CHAPTER NINE

MY SECOND WEEK of classes at Shelfbrooke Academy are almost exactly like the first one. People don't talk to me, and the work is too easy. I guess it could be worse, I tell myself, as I get dressed one Monday morning while my cousin lounges in her pajamas, half asleep in her bed.

The other students could go out of their way to be rude to me. But they don't. They just ignore me. My Cali friends aren't exactly ignoring me, but they don't seem to care about me now that I'm gone. Out of sight, out of mind. I text Viv every so often but she's not the kind of friend you want to text with. She's more of a friend you hang out with in person. She's there when you want to have a good time or share gossip. When you're stuck at a boarding school all the way across the country? She's not so available.

After that night in the gardens, I thought Declan might become something like a friend, but he's also ignored me every day since then. In chemistry, we haven't had to partner up again, but I also have him in English and history. Oh well. I'm fine without him. I am fine alone.

I leave the dorm bright and early and swing by the dining room to grab a coffee. Then, I take it to my favorite place—the gardens. Every morning I get a coffee and drink it here before it's time to go to class. I know it sounds silly, but it energizes me. Walking through the gorgeous gardens and being surrounded by nature makes me feel like I can take on the day.

All of those happy, warm feelings go away the second first period starts.

"Everyone pair up," the teacher says, waving his finger in a circle in the air. "This month we're doing a group project. Two people only, no groups of threes."

I don't even want to glance around the classroom and try to make eye contact with someone, anyone, who might have pity on me. I know it's useless. I prepare myself for a day of humiliation.

And then someone sits next to me. "Need a partner?"

He's short for a guy, with dirty blonde hair and dark eyes that look like they're hiding something. His uniform is wrinkled.

"I guess," I say, not exactly thrilled at the way he's looking at me, but happy that I'm not alone.

"Cool." He leans back in his chair and chews on the end of his pen. "You're the type who will do all the work, right?"

"Er..."

"Beat it," Declan says. He drops his textbook on the desktop with a loud thump. "She's my partner."

This guy, whoever he is, scowls up at Declan. "I got to her first."

Declan doesn't back down. Instead, he squares his shoulders. "I don't care."

The guy looks at me, and then back at Declan and shrugs. "Whatever, man."

He leaves, quickly joining another girl at the front of the class. Declan takes his spot. I want to thank him so badly, but my defenses are up, as always, and it's so much easier to be sarcastic than humble.

"Wow... two rescues in a row. You some kind of knight in shining armor?"

"My armor isn't very shiny," he says.

At the front of the class, the teacher explains our project. We're supposed to spend two weeks researching a topic that he provides, and then another two weeks writing an essay on it. We're supposed to do equal work with our partner and state each person's contribution on the last page of our essay. The teacher walks around handing out little slips of paper with a topic on it. Whatever it says, that's our project topic.

I'm nervous when the slip of paper drops on Declan's desk. He turns it over and I lean close to read it, catching the smell of his cologne at the same time. He always smells like summer, and it reminds me of home.

Social and political propaganda in literature

"Easy enough," I say.

Declan nods. "Wanna head to the library?"

"I don't think we can just get up and—" I say, but as I look around, I notice that half the class has already done just that. The teacher did say we'd be spending two weeks in the library. It's one building I haven't seen inside of yet, but from the outside, it's a stunning show of New England architecture.

I grab my bag and smile. "Let's go."

WHILE SCHOOL IS STILL awful and I still hate just about all of it, my first period English class is the best part of my day. For the next few days, I meet Declan in the library, way in the back at a small table that only has two chairs. It's a perfect place to hide out from the glares of my classmates and focus on our project.

It turns out that Declan isn't just a friendly student who is nice to look at. He's also incredibly smart. We make easy work of splitting up the project and then dividing off to research our parts. We have a shared document online where we keep our work in progress, and each day we both add to it. We don't really talk much in person, but we work well together. He focuses on his work, so I focus on mine. The worst part is when the bell rings and English class is over.

Because even though Declan has shown me kindness, no one else has. I've also just given up on the idea of trying to make friends with people. Now all I want to do is make it through the rest of the year as fast as possible, graduate, and go back home.

"I loved your line about corporate shills," Declan says as we pack up our stuff at the end of class.

"Thanks," I say, tucking my hair behind my ear. "I was proud of that line."

"I'm going to write a few pages tonight. You should read over them later and see if anything I said sounds stupid."

"I will." I slide my laptop into my back and sling it

over my shoulder. "And you can point out anything in my passages that sounds off, too."

Declan sucks in air through his teeth. "I'll try, but your writing is pretty perfect already."

A subtle warmth spreads through my chest at his kind comment. When he says stuff like that, the teensy little secret crush I'm harboring over him seems to grow tenfold. But I tuck it back down. There's no reason to crush on some random Shelfbrooke guy. As soon as I cross the stage at graduation, I am so out of here.

A couple of Declan's friends say hi to him in the hallway, so I take the opportunity to slip off by myself and head to my next class. No need to obligate him to walk with me any longer than necessary. I eat lunch with Belle in our dorm, which is now our tradition. The dining hall is a beautiful building, but I've only stepped foot in there to grab my food as quickly as possible and then walk back to the dorm. Before I arrived, Belle's lunch was delivered by a lunch lady each day. Now I just pick it up and bring it to her. I'm pretty sure that one lunch lady was the only human contact she's had for most of her school life. My aunt stops by on occasion, but she doesn't really count because she's Belle's mom.

When the weather is nice, I've also settled into my favorite after school routine: the gardens. I now know the simple way through the paths, the largest most walked paths where I got lost that night when Declan rescued me. But I also know smaller, less-used pathways too. I have a few favorite spots, little off the path places to sit and be surrounded by the beauty of nature and the tall, lush greenery that makes up the garden's walls. As long as it's not raining, I spend my evenings here, sitting on a blanket or a concrete bench with my laptop and my homework.

Like my cousin, I've become sort of a hermit too, in a way. I go outside but I keep to myself. I bet my Cali friends wouldn't even recognize me now. Oh well. This is what I have to do to survive. I am done trying to make friends when the whole school just ignores me.

As I settle down on my black and red plaid blanket, my parents cross my mind. And then I roll my eyes and try to forget about them. My mom hasn't called me once in the last two weeks. Dad tagged me in one of his online posts, which I guess is his form of acknowledging that I exist, even if it was on a tweet about some news story he found hilarious. My parents don't care about me. And if they don't care about me, then I won't care about them.

Ironically, the only person who does check on me every few days is my Aunt Kate. She calls and makes sure I'm doing alright, and of course, I always lie and say I'm fine.

I open my laptop and tell myself to focus. I will not

let the pain of being unloved by my own parents bother me today. I won't think about the Shelfbrooke kids and how they don't talk to me. I won't think about Viv, and the five unread Snapchat messages I've sent her this week.

I pull up the essay I share with Declan online. It's saved in the school's cloud-based server, so Declan and I can both work on it at the same time. The little icon in the top corner tells me he's also logged in right now, working on the essay. Since we have split up the work evenly, he writes some pages, and I write others.

A message pops up on the screen. I didn't realize this document website had a chat feature.

Declan: Someone isn't pulling their weight with this project.

I lift an eyebrow and type back.

Sophia: Excuse me?

Declan: I checked the word count. I've written 4081 words and you've written 4044 words. Tisk tisk, Sophia...

I grin, and think of a comeback.

Sophia: I shouldn't be punished for my ability to eloquently state facts without extraneous words.

Declan: Ouch. Insulting my intelligence... Hold on

a minute while I delete 38 words... There we go. I am now one word more efficient than you.

I throw my head back and laugh.

"Sophia?"

I freeze. That was Declan's voice I just heard, coming from the other side of the garden wall. "Declan?" I call back.

A few moments later, he appears, laptop tucked underneath his arm. He's wearing his Shelfbrooke uniform because the rules state that they must be worn on campus at all times.

I, however, how know to sneak the short distance from the staff dorms to the gardens without being seen. And once I'm behind the garden walls, it doesn't matter what I wear. So I'm in jeans and a Harvard sweatshirt. Still, even in uniform, the boy is really attractive. I swallow.

"What are you doing here?"

"Me?" Declan says, putting a hand to his chest. A little dimple appears in his right cheek when he smiles. "These are my gardens. I'm always here. The question is what are you doing here?"

I shrug and slide over on the blanket, offering him the spot next to me. "This is my sanctuary."

"Sanctuary..." he says, settling down next to me. "I like that. All my hard work that keeps this garden looking beautiful has clearly paid off." He brings the smell of his cologne with him and it makes my heart race. He smells so deliciously like summer and boy, and I wish I could breathe him in all the time.

"How much of this is your work?" I ask.

He gazes up at the pink rose bush across the pathway. "A lot. But if you count my family history, then most of it can be attributed to the Moss Family."

"What do you mean?"

He opens his laptop and logs in. "My family made these gardens from the roots up. A few generations ago. They were hired as the gardeners, and they grew and tended to the gardens. The labyrinth was the creation of my great-grandfather. My family's soul and blood and sweat are in these gardens."

"Wow," I say. "So you're related to the other gardeners I see around campus?"

His expression darkens, his lips pressing together. "No. A few years ago, one of the Big Five took over the school board—"

"Big Five?" I say.

"The five most prominent families around here. Their kids are the meanest, most entitled students here."

"Ah," I say with a nod. "I think I've seen some of them."

He snorts. "Well, the school board changed, and

they took over the gardens. They didn't want to pay my dad's company, which was the same company passed down through my family each generation, and instead they hired outside gardeners. But my dad needed a job, so he got hired on by the new company. You should have seen it. Within six months, this place completely fell apart." He shakes his head and exhales. "Companies who hire random people with no gardening knowledge and tell them to garden, well, it was a disaster. My dad worked so hard to get the gardens back to where they should be, and as soon as I turned sixteen and could legally work, I got a job here, too. Even if the gardens aren't officially my family's any more, I can't let them get ruined. They're a Shelfbrooke tradition."

I look over at him. "I'm sorry I made fun of you for being a gardener the day I met you."

He shrugs. "You wouldn't be the first."

The sound of voices makes us both look up. Three senior girls who I recognize from my classes turn the corner and walk down the path that's right in front of us. They're talking about some girl named Amber and how she has bad skin. Then they see us, and their conversation immediately stops.

I look at my computer and type a few words of nonsense, just so I look busy.

They stay silent as they walk past us, and when I glance up to see if they're gone, Declan is looking, too.

"Why is everyone so mean here?" I whisper, just in case anyone else is around.

He shrugs. "People are mean everywhere, Sophia. You just have to find the nice ones and surround yourself with them."

CHAPTER TEN

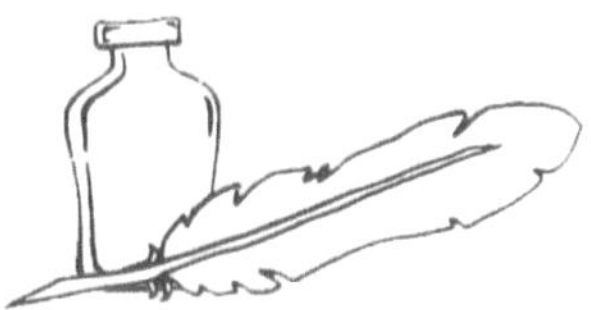

THERE'S a little pep in my step as I walk back to my dorm after an afternoon spent sitting next to Declan in the gardens. I feel like we became friends today. Not just partners, or acquaintances, but actual friends. And there's nothing wrong with having an incredibly attractive friend.

I do the little familiar knock I've invented on our dorm door just before I unlock it and let myself in. Doing the same knock each day calms Belle's nerves because she knows it's me. I still think it's weird that she gets scared of the idea of a stranger being at the door, especially since her traumatic episode didn't involve anyone hurting her. But her panic attacks are her thing, and I'm trying to make it easy on her. I'm pretty sure she could go tell the administration if she wanted me gone, and they'd send me to live with two roommates in the real dorms where they have shared bathrooms. No thanks.

"You look happy," Belle says. Like always, she's sitting on her bed, on the computer.

I shrug. "This lock is getting easier and easier every day. It just needed a little elbow grease to make it work."

"That's not why you're happy," she says. "You look happy for other reasons. Boy reasons, perhaps?"

"What kind of nonsense are you going on about?" I toss my bag and plug my laptop into the charger and then steal a bag of Skittles from Belle's bookshelf candy stash.

"I'm talking about Declan."

"He's just a friend. A classmate."

"A *romantic* classmate?" Belle says, grinning at me like a kid who just saw their parents kissing.

I throw a Skittle at her. "No! What's gotten into you?"

She turns the laptop around and I briefly see a photo on the screen. It's me, in my Harvard sweatshirt, and Declan in his school uniform. The photo was taken from behind us, secretly, because I definitely didn't know about it. It shows us walking next to each other just as the sun is getting low on the horizon. That must have been taken ten minutes ago.

"What kind of stalker crap is that?" I say, diving onto her bed.

She quickly closes her laptop. "Someone posted it to Knight Watch. There's a rumor going around that you and Declan are a thing."

"I want to see it," I say, making grabby hands.

Her hands fold over the top of the laptop and she tugs it toward her. "It's not a big deal."

My lips press into a tight line. "That means it is a big deal."

I haven't signed up for Knight Watch yet because I haven't seen a need in looking at school-specific social media page. It's not like I have any friends to add on there, and it's not like I have anything to say. Plus, my own social media accounts have pretty much gone ignored since I was forced to move here against my will. I have nothing to share with the world while I'm stuck in this boarding school.

Still, Belle doesn't know that. "I'll just make my own profile and see for myself," I say.

She rolls her eyes. "Fine. But you can't get upset because I tried to protect you from this."

She slides the computer over and I open it, looking once again at that photo of Declan and me.

A: looks like someone is getting cozy with the Cali brat.

"Who is A?" I say, clicking on the little circle with the letter in the middle of it. Nothing comes up.

"It's anonymous. You can post as yourself, or anonymously."

"Awesome," I say sarcastically. Then I read the comments below. Some of them are posted by anonymous accounts and others are using their real names. But it's not like I know any of these people, so I don't pay attention to the names.

Someone tell him he doesn't have to take pity on the new girl.

Ugh, Declan Moss is too nice. Like, so nice it makes him slightly less hot.

Didn't he get the memo that We Hate Her?

Quick, someone tell him!

I skim over the comments, trying not to grow angry at them in front of Belle. I don't want to prove her right, after all. Then, I see Declan's name pop up. He's just left a comment.

Declan: She's my English project partner, guys. Chill out.

I frown. So that's what I am. That's *all* I am. All these days of flirty comments in our shared essay document. Today at the gardens, talking about his family and his love of gardening. Me, laughing and enjoying his company. It was all just nothing.

We're just partners. He couldn't bother saying: *She's actually nice. She's cool. She's my friend.*

Of course not.

I know Belle is reading over my shoulder, so there's no point in showing her Declan's new comment.

"See?" I say. "It's nothing. We're just friends."

The screen refreshes with dozens of new posts to the

main feed. Someone is clearly trying to get their message heard because there's gifs of people dancing and flailing and confetti.

PARTY ALERT

Belle and I watch and read the screen as more information is posted.

Party tonight in Kingsbere Hall. Upperclassmen only. Sorry, kiddos. All cool peeps are invited! We've got that DJ from the pizzeria spinning some jams tonight. Be there or be square!

A person by the name of Mikey posts: *Cool kids are invited? Am I on that list?*

You know it

Of course, bro! If you're cool, you're invited!

Dozens of new replies show up faster than I can keep track of them as the homepage reloads. Most people are just excited about the party. A few underclassmen complain that none of the good parties allow them to go.

Someone named Brady says he's a band nerd and wonders if he qualifies under the 'cool kids only' rule. Someone replies yes, he's invited.

I get bored and realize I'm glad I didn't make myself a profile on there. It's all just stupid social media crap that doesn't matter. I'm happier not knowing anything about it.

"Look at this," Sophia says a few minutes later. For not wanting to socialize with anyone in person, the girl really loves looking at Knight Watch. Her eyes go wide. "You're invited."

"What?"

She points to the screen and I read over it.

Someone should invite Declan's new girlfriend.

Seriously? We're inviting spoiled California heiresses now?

Why not? All the other spoiled east coast heiresses are invited. XD

"Why are these people so obsessed with me?" I say, throwing my hands in the air.

"Because you're the new girl," Belle says. "They need someone to talk about. Trust me, it's always someone getting anonymously talked about on here. Today it's you, but they'll move on to someone else soon.

"Maybe I should go to that party," I muse.

"It didn't really work out for you last time though."

"Last time was ... stupid," I say, unable to come up with a better adjective. "It's been a couple weeks and Declan has warmed up to me. Maybe other people will, too. Plus, I'm tired of sitting in this dorm every single day. No offense."

My cousin doesn't look affected by my off-hand comment. She lays down on her side, still watching her computer. "If you want to, go for it."

My lips spread into a grin. "I think I will," I say. "What should I wear?"

DÉJÀ VU SWEEPS over me as I make my way down to Kingsbere Hall for the second time in as many weeks. I try not to think about that first night, when I was clueless and fell apart at a couple of snide comments from random girls. That won't happen now. I'm the talk of the school, clearly, and they said they wanted me to come. Well, at least someone with an Anonymous A next to their name said that. Plus, this party is open to lots of people this time. My dad always says that success is given to people who reach out and take it, again and again, without letting a few failures stop them.

Tonight is my version of reaching out. I like my cousin, but I don't like spending all my time with her. I need to make new friends.

There are two rather large senior guys standing at the doors of Kingsbere Hall. They're not in uniform, but some of the students walking into the building are still wearing the annoying school-issued clothing.

"Upperclassmen only," the guy on the left says, tossing his thumb out. "Get out of here, kid."

A short, wiry boy who is so very clearly a freshman groans and turns around. I guess he thought it was worth a shot to try to sneak into the party. I fall into the makeshift line behind a few people who don't pay any attention to me. This is great. If I'm not noticed, I can blend in. I can finally start making friends.

The people in front of me are let into the old building without a word. The two guys close the door when I walk up.

"You're not invited," the guy on the left says.

"I'm an upperclassman," I say, putting on a smile. "A senior, actually."

"I don't care what grade you're in, Brass. You're not invited."

I glance at the other guy, but he just folds his arms over his chest and stares at me, emotionless.

I open my mouth to speak, then close it again. Are they joking? Is it some friendly hazing to the new girl?

The first guy claps once in my face. "Why are you still here?"

The old me, the girl in Cali, would have never put up with this kind of disrespect. But I'm so thrown off guard here, that I just step backward, and turn around. That's when I see Declan, walking up with two guys about our age. His eyes meet mine for a split second and then he looks at the two guys who are self-imposed bouncers for this event.

The guy who just yelled at me glances at Declan and his friends, nods once, and steps aside. "You're good."

"Anyone wanna vouch for this chick?" the other door guy says. "She wants in, but she's not invited."

Declan doesn't even look at me. He just walks into the building. My heart breaks open at his epic betrayal. I thought we were friends.

The other two guys hang back a bit, eyeing me up and down. I stand straight, feeling like a complete loser for hoping they say I should be let into the party.

"Nah," the of the guys says. "I ain't messing with the new girl."

"Yeah, leave me out of that," the other guy says.

I turn around and walk as fast as I can. Clearly, I'm not welcome at this school. So why do I keep stupidly trying to make friends with these people?

And why did the only person who's shown me kindness just act like I don't even exist?

CHAPTER ELEVEN

I WILL NOT CRY. I will not cry. I will not cry.

I can handle being the butt of some online jokes. I can handle having people turn away from me when the teachers want group work. But Declan was my friend. At least, I thought he was. And tonight he pretended I didn't even exist.

My whole body feels heavy, weary with the humiliation and realization that nothing is what I thought it was. My black sparkly flats glisten under the moonlight and the soft glow of each street lamp as I pass under it on my walk back to the dorms.

As much as I want to hate Declan, I'm not sure I can blame him for wanting nothing to do with me. Everyone else doesn't like me. I wish he had just been more upfront about it, instead of pretending to be nice to me while we worked on our English project.

Yeah, well the truth is out now. Next time a teacher tells us to partner up, I'm going to stand up and walk back to my dorm. If they let Belle do her school work online, they'll just have to let me do it, too. I'm not going to sit here and be humiliated repeatedly for the next few months.

I keep trying to get myself angry. Anger is easier than sorrow. I want to hate Declan. Hate the students at Shelfbrooke. I don't want to be sad.

But sadness keeps leeching onto me anyhow. It crawls up my legs and wraps around my heart and squeezes until all I want to do is drop into a ball and cry.

I turn onto the pathway that leads to the staff dorms, and then I stop short. It's only been fifteen minutes since I left my dorm, all dressed up with hair I spent an hour curling and makeup I spent another hour applying. Belle was excited for me, too. She told me to have fun and make friends and do all the things she can't do since she's unable to leave our room.

Going back home now would just disappoint her and show how truly pathetic I am. My hands clench into fists and I turn on my heel, walking away from the dorms, but in the opposite direction of the party.

I go to the gardens.

Shelfbrooke piles so much school work on its students that we rarely have free time. And when I am done with my homework, I usually hang out with Belle, or sit in the gardens and try to relax. I haven't done much exploring, especially after I memorized the pathways that are on the outer banks of the gardens. I can get from one end to the other, using the same paths each time, but I've never ventured further into the masterfully designed walls that create a labyrinth of beautiful flowers and plants that stretch on for acres.

Tonight, that changes.

I refuse to cry here, not in the first garden. Not near the stone statues that students love to pose in front of for selfies. I can't cry anywhere that might have other students lurking nearby. I need to go further.

I stick to the south wall of the garden, where the moonlight shines brightly down a long pathway that's devoid of any of the beautiful showy flowers that the west side of the garden has. Here, it's just two tall walls of vines with a cobblestone walkway between them. I walk for ten minutes, then twenty.

I only take a couple of turns, when it looks like the pathway ahead of me turns into a dead end.

The glow of the campus lights don't reach this far into the gardens. I have only the moonlight to guide me, and the dark shadows that indicate another pathway up ahead. Perhaps on another day, this might be a little frightening, wandering around in the dark, with no clue where I am.

But tonight it feels freeing.

I am not afraid of the dark.

I used to be afraid of being alone, but right now it doesn't seem so bad. No one can hurt you when you are alone.

I turn and amble slowly down new pathways, my fingers skittering over the petals of flowers as I pass them. I lose track of which turn I take, which direction is back home. I don't really care anymore. The gardens make a perfect refuge.

A soft beep fills the air. At first I think it's my phone, but then the sound happens again, and it's definitely not coming from my pocket.

"Are you seriously going to check your phone right now?" a guy says.

"Sorry," a softer voice says back. "I'll turn it off."

"Good. Now where were we?"

Ew!

I make a sharp turn and walk in the opposite direction so I don't stumble upon whatever that couple was doing back there. Clearly, I'm not far enough into the gardens to fully lose myself and everyone else.

I keep walking.

I walk until my feet start to hurt because these adorable ballet flats are just that—adorable. They aren't comfortable or meant to be walked in for so long. I find an old wooden bench that looks like it hasn't been used in decades and I sit down and pull off my shoes to let my feet have a break. The moonlight is right overhead now, lighting up a good bit of the area around me. I think my eyes have adjusted to the darkness, because it's not so dark anymore. I take out my phone and scroll through social media. I haven't made a single post since I moved here three weeks ago.

And no one has noticed.

My Cali friends are still posting their normal stuff. Parties, shopping sprees, photos on private planes. Normally I would be included in these photos, but now I'm not, and no one seems to care.

I read through some comments, and not one person asks where Sophia is. Even Viv has gone on posting a few times a day like her life is exactly the same.

Does anyone, anywhere care about me?

My eyes sting with a fresh round of sorrow. I blink a few times and refuse to cry.

My nannies and caretakers over the years have always told me I have a charmed life. That I'm spoiled, loved, favored. That I'll never know what real work is. And maybe that last part is true thanks to my trust fund.

Maybe I am just a stuck-up brat who has everything given to her.

But this life doesn't feel very charmed right now.

I keep thinking about Declan, even though I don't want to. I keep replaying that first day we met, how I treated him like garbage. It wasn't his fault. He didn't deserve any of it. I was just mad that I was being sent to this school. I should have been nicer. Maybe we'd be real friends now, instead of fake ones.

A small bird drops down beside me on the bench. It's too dark to make out what kind of bird it is, but it's cute.

"Hello," I say softly.

The bird looks up at me, or at least I think it does. It chirps a soft sound.

"How are you?" I ask, my sorrow temporarily forgotten.

It chirps again.

I hold out my hand, slowly, and the little bird jumps into my palm. I almost squeal in surprise, because I hadn't expected that. But I hold still, trying not to scare it. This is some serious Disney princess stuff right here.

"Do you want to be my friend?" I ask, my voice so soft I barely hear it. I know it's stupid to talk to a bird. I know it's pathetic to ask a tiny little animal to be my friend. But it's not like anyone is around to witness it.

The bird chirps again, and then it jumps up, flying in the air above me for a just a moment. "Where are you going?" I ask.

And then it flies straight at the vine wall in front me. I gasp as it disappears.

It straight up disappears!

"How in the—" I stand up and walk toward the garden wall. The bird couldn't have disappeared, I tell myself. It only looked like it did. Maybe it's right there inside the green garden wall. I reach out slowly and feel the lush greenery in front of me. The leaves are only a few inches thick, and then there's a solid wall behind it.

Curious, I press harder, then I pull the leaves apart. The rest of the garden walls aren't really walls—they are just really high bushes that are trimmed into wall shapes. You could get a pair of garden shears and cut your way through the walls if you wanted.

But this is very much a *real* wall. Brick, by the feel of it. It's a real wall covered in vines that make it look like any other garden wall.

And that makes the bird's disappearance even more of a mystery. I spread my hands out, gently pressing against the vines and leaves, feeling a hard wall behind every single place I touch.

Curious, I walk several steps one way, pressing the wall every so often. After about ten feet, the wall gives, and it's a bush once again. I backtrack, finding where the brick wall starts. I walk all the way down the opposite direction and do the same thing.

The hidden brick wall is about the length of my dorm room. I gaze up. It's only about seven feet tall, but seeing as I'm five feet, three inches, there's no way I can see over it. Curiosity takes over me though, and I want to know what this wall is. Is it just some monument? Maybe a decoration that's been taken over by the gardens? Or is it something special?

I don't know why I feel this way, but I would bet all my luxury handbags that this isn't just some wall. It's special. I can feel it deep in my soul.

The bird appears again, flying just over my shoulder.

"There you are!" I say, taking a step back. I pull out my cell phone and turn on the flashlight. "Where did you go?"

The bird is blue, with yellow on its head, and it has a cute little round belly. The bird heads straight toward the wall again, but this time my light is shining on it. I watch him disappear. Then I bring the light closer to the exact spot.

And it's open. A fragrant smell of roses fills the air when I lean against the wall, against this small opening. I can't see anything, can't get a better idea of what's behind that hole without damaging the vines. That's when I realize the earthy smell coming from the wall reminds me of the wooden bench I was just sitting on a few minutes ago.

I take a step back, then knock on the wall. It's wooden.

This is a door.

The rest of the hidden wall is brick, but this isn't. I feel around, scrambling to find the handle, the opening, that will reveal what's behind the door. But it's too dark, and my phone is flashing the low battery warning at me.

It's just after three in the morning. If I were to get caught outside this late at night, I'd definitely get into trouble.

With a sigh, I turn off my phone's flashlight and fall into darkness once again. Opening the GPS app on my phone, I drop a pin on the screen, marking this exact location in the gardens. The GPS obviously doesn't have the gardens marked like it has the public roads, so the area on the map is just solid green. But now I have at least a slight idea of how to get back here in the morning.

I yawn and turn around, pocketing my phone before it dies. I have no idea what lies behind that hidden door.

But as soon as the sun rises, I'm going to figure it out.

CHAPTER TWELVE

AUNT KATE COMES over bright and early on Saturday morning. Normally I'd be happy to see her, and thrilled that she brought us a huge order of bagels, five flavors of cream cheese, and coffee from The Pure Drop coffee shop in town. But this morning is not a normal morning because I got home so late last night.

It was so late, in fact, that my cousin had fallen asleep watching Netflix on her computer and the volume was on so she didn't even hear me get back to our dorm. I quickly changed clothes and went to bed exhausted at four in the morning, only to get woken up a few hours later.

As far as Belle knows, I went to the party last night. I don't want to tell anyone what I actually did, because now, in the bright sunlight of a fresh new day, with the smell of coffee and fresh bagels in the room, it feels really dumb to have spent hours wandering in the gardens, thinking I'd found a secret door. It was probably just a storage shed for rakes or something.

I yawn and thank Aunt Kate for the surprise breakfast. She asks how school is going and I lie and tell her it's going well. She then asks Belle the same thing, and she gives the same answer. But Belle doesn't seem like she's lying to appease her mom. Despite doing all her school work in our dorm, I think Belle truly believes things are going well. She's been cooped up in her dorm for so long that she no longer thinks it's a problem. I want to ask my aunt what will happen when Belle graduates this summer. She might be able to take college classes online, and then even get a job online after that, but that's no life to live. I want her to see the beauty the world has to offer. Now that Belle and I are friends I want to take her to the gardens, or to Malibu to hang out at my pool, or on the beach. She'll never get to do any of that if she doesn't find a way to go outside.

Just like every time I think of this problem, I know it's not the time to bring it up. So I eat my breakfast and participate in the fun small talk, and don't say anything that will rock the boat.

My aunt leaves a short while later with a list of things Belle needs from the store, like shampoo and hair ties. It occurs to me that I haven't left the campus myself since I got here. All the things I've needed so far, I just ordered from Amazon and had shipped to the school. In a weird way, I've become a hermit, too. Only it's the school grounds holding me inside instead of the dorm.

"I'm going outside," I say, standing up and reaching for yesterday's school uniform. It's a weekend, but the stupid rules say we still have to wear them on campus.

"Where are you going?" Belle asks. She's still in her pajamas, which is what she wears just about every day.

"I don't know. Just out. I might call an Uber to take me somewhere."

"Cool," she says, seeming disinterested.

I tug on my clothes and run a brush through my hair quickly, before pulling it up into a bun. "You should come with me."

She chuckles. "Ha *ha*," she says sarcastically.

"I'm serious." I stop at the door and turn to face her. "We could walk in the gardens."

"I wish I could," she says, and there's a finality in her voice that tells me to leave it be. So I do.

I have every intention of walking to the main entrance and calling one of those Uber rideshare things to take me into town, but once I pull up my phone to download the app, the GPS app is still loaded from last night. I see the marker I saved that's deep in the gardens, and a curiosity starts tugging at me. Was that really a door? What's inside of it?

I need to know.

Turning into the gardens, I skim the pathways for any students and I turn away when I see some. I follow the marker on my GPS, but I can't exactly walk straight to it because of the pathways.

My heart beats faster as I approach it, and some of the pathways seem vaguely familiar. With the sun shining brightly overhead, everything looks different. It's beautiful out here, lush and green even though we're in the start of February. The flowers are a beautiful array of pinks and reds and whites.

My heart almost stops when I turn a corner and see an old wooden bench. That's the bench I sat on last night. Running up to the opposite wall, I stop right in front of it and stare up. It looks just like any other garden wall—covered in ivy with thick green leaves.

I press my hand to it, almost expecting last night to be a dream. I almost wish it was, because if last night didn't actually happen, then Declan never betrayed me.

My hand touches the soft, slightly chilly wood surface beneath the vines. This door is real. And Declan is still a jerk.

I feel around, the wooden surface easy to see between the vines now that it's daylight. I reach the spot where the wood ends and the brick wall begins. I move my fingers down, down, until they hit an old rusted hinge.

I move to the other side of the door, looking for a handle. There has to be one.

And there is.

My heart pounds as I uncover an old metal handle, vines wrapped around it. I grab it and pull. It doesn't even budge. It doesn't groan or creak or wiggle at all. It is completely stuck.

No, not suck. Locked.

I brush away some of the vines, careful not to pull apart too many which would reveal this location to anyone else who happens to walk by.

Sure enough, right above the handle is a metal lock, with a big opening like an old skeleton key should fit in there. I bend over and peer into the hole, hoping to see something, anything, on the other side, but it's dark.

My little bird friend is gone today, but I search for the hole in the door that he had flown through, and find a design that looks like it maybe used to have stained glass in it or something. Now it's hollow, a little circle hole in the top of the door. The vines are thick, and the hole is just high enough that I can barely see it if I stand on my tip-toes. I peer inside.

All the air rushes out of my lungs.

It's bright inside there. Green, and pink and purple and white, white like marble? I'm not sure. The fragrant flower smell is the sweetest I've experienced, even better than walking through the normal parts of the gardens. Whatever is behind this door is a hundred times better than the gardens out here. I just know it. I can feel it.

I drop down on my feet and grab the door handle again, anxious and desperate to get inside.

I brush away more vines, wondering if I can somehow pick the lock, despite having no lock-picking skills at all.

And then I see it.

An old silver emblem mounted into the wood, just above the lock. The once-shiny metal is now brown from the elements, but the symbol is still there, easy to see. I run my fingers over the intricate curves, the familiar design making all the heartache of last night come back to me full force.

The symbol on this lock is the same symbol on the pendant around Declan's neck.

If there's a key to this hidden paradise, Declan will know how to find it.

CHAPTER THIRTEEN

I SPEND the rest of the weekend in my room with Belle, but when Monday comes, I know I have to drag myself out of this dorm and the safety of Netflix marathons with my cousin and face the real world again. I used to get annoyed and even a little resentful that I had to leave and face a student body that hates me and she got to stay home.

But now I just feel sad for my sweet cousin. Her crippling anxiety is like a prison, holding her in one place and not letting her move. I pull my shoes on and then turn to face her.

"There's a hidden part of the gardens."

She sits up on her elbow, blinking away the morning sunlight that filters in through the lone window in our room. "What do you mean hidden?"

"It's like... a secret place. No one goes out there. But it's beautiful. It's mysterious. Surrounded by flowers and sweet little birds that fly up to you."

Belle sits up and kicks the blanket off, her eyes wide open now. "You've been there?"

"Yes," I say. "It took me hours to find it, and I know how to get back."

I'm stretching the truth, but I can't help it. I mean, yes there is a hidden part of the garden, and I know how to get there. But I can't get inside. But it's not like it matters, right? Belle will never know the difference, which means I can just entertain her with my story of a beautiful place she'll never see.

"I want to see it," Belle says.

"I'll take some pictures for you."

"No..." she stands up, slipping her feet into her plaid house shoes. "I want to actually see it."

My jaw drops. "Now?"

"Well... no," Belle admits, her teeth wearing into her bottom lip. "It's before school and there will be people everywhere..." She thinks for a moment, and I just can't believe what I'm hearing.

"What about later?" Belle says, glancing out the window. "Maybe at night where no one would see me. You said you can get around the campus without being seen. Can you take me?"

My jaw works, but it takes me a second to find the words to speak. "Um... Yeah. I mean, yes, I can. Are you sure?"

She nods, her gaze still out the window as the early morning sun shines through. "I've been thinking about what you said. About graduation and what I'll do after. You're right—I can't stay here. I can't just stay here forever."

"This is great news, Belle."

She nods softly then walks to the front door. "I just need to get over my anxiety and just...do it."

She twists the deadbolt, her fingers moving very slowly, but finally the door clicks and it's unlocked. She reaches for the door handle. I have about five minutes to jog across campus and get to my first class before the late bell rings, so I shoulder my backpack and meet her at the door.

"What are you doing?"

"I'm going to step outside," she says, standing tall and confident. Her hand shakes, but she twists the doorknob and opens it a few inches. This part isn't a big deal. She opens the door all the time, to let me or her mom inside. It's what comes after that that's worrying me.

With the door open, Belle takes a deep, ragged breath.

"Will you see if anyone is out there?" she whispers.

I step into the hallway and look both ways. Like always, it's empty. I've only seen two teachers who actually live in these dorms, and their rooms are at the end of the hall. They're probably already in their classrooms since school is about to start.

"It's clear," I say.

Belle nods, then slides her foot forward. It's like she doesn't want to take a real step, but she's comfortable inching forward with her feet still firmly on the floor.

She exhales, then does it again.

I'm anxious about the clock, knowing I will be late if I don't leave soon, but this is a big deal. I can't just leave her. For the first time in three years, Belle is stepping out of the dorm.

Guess I'll just have to be late to class.

"Are you sure no one is out there?" she asks. I make a big deal about looking left and right, as I stand in the hallway and then I nod. "All clear."

She closes her eyes, then takes one step forward. Her whole body is in the hallway now.

"You did it," I say.

"I did it!" she says, her voice on the verge of an excited shriek. She looks around and then bounces on her toes. "I'm going to touch the wall."

I lift an eyebrow, but my cousin doesn't seem to think her new goal is weird. She takes three strides forward and then reaches out and presses her hand to the wall. She turns to me and blows out a breath. "Wow."

"You did great," I say. I check the time on my phone.

"You should get going," Belle says. "I don't want you to get in trouble because of me."

"Are you sure?" I put away my phone. "We can walk down the hall if you want."

"That's okay," she says, quickly scaling the small space and walking back into our dorm. "I've had enough excitement for a while. But maybe tonight you can take me."

"Take you where?" I ask suspiciously.

"The hidden garden."

"Oh. Okay." Crap. I nod and put on a fake smile. "Sure."

Belle's cheeks flush with happiness and she clasps her hands together in front of her chest. "I'm so excited. You can get us there with no one seeing us, right?"

"Yes," I say, confident in at least that part. I've become something of an expert at sneaking around campus with no one noticing me.

"Perfect." She makes a shooing motion with her hand. "Now get to class!"

I AM POSITIVELY FREAKING OUT. My cousin made a huge stride in overcoming her anxiety today all because I told her about a place I technically can't get into. And now tonight she wants me to take her there.

Visions of making a trip to the hardware store for a saw or a crowbar taunt me as I run across campus toward Kellylynch Hall. I couldn't do that to my beloved gardens. Breaking open the door would ruin everything. But how can I get in without a key?

The bell is ringing right as I slip into class, out of breath from running up three flights of stairs. But I technically made it here right on time. The teacher gives me the stink eye but doesn't say anything as I slip into my seat at the back of the classroom.

It's a new week which means the start of another project, but luckily fate has blessed me because we're told it's a solo project. No partners required.

I keep to myself as we make our way down to the library to begin research on a personal essay of our choosing. When Declan glances at me from across the room, my anger rises up and makes me look away. I still can't believe he did that to me at the party last weekend. And, now that I'm mad at him, I can't exactly ask about his necklace and if he knows where the key to the hidden garden might be. No, I refuse to talk to him.

So I'll have to figure this out on my own.

I start my research by looking into the books about Shelfbrooke Academy's history. I'm hoping that the symbol that's above the garden door lock and on Declan's necklace will be explained. Maybe I'll even find out where Shelfbrooke keeps old artifacts. Maybe I'll get lucky and find a book called *Old Keys of Shelfbrooke and Where To Find Them*.

I chuckle to myself and keep searching the library. By the end of the class period, I've skimmed every single history book there is, including a few biographies of previous school deans, but I've got nothing when it comes to the gardens. The only thing the history books seem to say about the gardens is that they're beautiful masterpieces that sprawl across several hundred acres. Only a few books mention Declan's grandfather as the head gardener and original designer. But there's absolutely nothing on the symbol.

I pack away my books and start to head out of the library, on my way to second period, when someone clears their throat behind me.

I know who it is. And I don't turn around.

"Sophia," Declan says, walking next to me despite being ignored. "Sophia, I want to talk."

I keep my eyes forward. "You want to talk? That's funny. Because you didn't want to talk at that party last week."

"Sophia," Declan says softer. "I can explain."

I turn the corner and slip into an alcove that has a large window overlooking the gardens. "Oh, please explain," I say with as much sarcasm as I can. "Please tell me why you acted like my friend for two weeks and then straight up betrayed me in front of those two jerks at the party."

"I know it looks bad," he says, running a hand through his dark hair. Those eyes of his still make my toes tingle when looks at me, but I grit my jaw and refuse to think about how cute he is. "I'm sorry. I couldn't do anything—" He sighs again, and he's either a really good actor, or this is actually bothering him. "I feel terrible. I hate myself for doing that to you."

My stone-cold façade fades a little. But I keep staring at him. "So explain," I snap.

He glances around. "It's Chad Stokes. He's one of the Big Five."

"The rich Shelfbrooke families?" I say, vaguely remembering the term Big Five. In Cali we don't have stupid phrases like that. Maybe because everyone is rich where I come from.

He nods. "He knows you. He knows you from Malibu and when he found out we were friends, he..." Declan shakes his head like he's embarrassed. "He threatened me. He said he'd take my job away. Said he'd have the entire gardens burned down if I didn't stay away. See, when you first got here, he sent a Knight Watch message to everyone. We were told not to befriend you."

"What?" My voice is louder than I intend. "Some guy tells everyone not talk to me, and they listened?"

He shrugs. "Maybe not everyone. Chad only talks to the elite of Shelfbrooke. The only people who *matter*," he says, rolling his eyes at the last word. They're the reason you're being shunned."

"But why?" I say. "I don't even know this guy."

Declan shrugs. "I don't know. I'm sorry, I really am. But he was right there and if I had said anything—I didn't want to lose my job, or the gardens..."

"It's fine," I say. "The gardens are special to me, too."

"I'm not like them," Declan says, a pained expression on his face. "I don't come from money. I get free tuition because of my grandfather's hard work. Outside of these gates, I'm just a regular guy. All the other students here are wealthy, and they know they're better than me."

"They're not better than you," I say.

My phone rings, which is odd since it's the middle of school and no one ever talks to me anymore. I look at the screen and see Belle's name. She wouldn't call me unless It was important.

"Sorry, I have to go."

Declan nods and apologizes again but I don't have time to think about what he just said and the implications it has on my social life here at Shelfbrooke Academy. I'm concerned about my cousin right now.

"Belle?" I say, answering my phone in a corner of the hallway so I don't get trampled by the other students.

"Come home," she says, her voice panicked. "Please come home."

"What's wrong?"

"Everything."

CHAPTER FOURTEEN

I SPRINT ACROSS CAMPUS, clutching my backpack to my chest so my laptop doesn't get broken in the process. Visions of Belle lying half dead on the floor fill my mind, even though I'm pretty sure she would have called 911 if that were the case. Still. I can't shake the frightened sound of her voice.

I almost knock into someone on my run, and hear a string of hurtful insults hurled my way, but there's no time to hiss something equally mean back to them. I don't know what kind of power this Stokes guy has over everyone here, but I refuse to let it bother me. Maybe he's just jealous that my life in Cali is better than his life here.

I yank open the door to our building and my shoes are loud against the flooring as I skid to a stop in front of door sixty-two. My hands shake as I reach for my key, but the door swings open before I unlock it.

"Finally," Belle says, one hand on the door and the other on her chest.

I step inside and she locks up the door behind me. I give her a once over and she looks intact. No blood or missing appendages. She's breathing loudly though, panting like she's the one who just ran a marathon instead of me.

"What's wrong?" I ask, grabbing her shoulders.

"It's... it's..." she gasps for breath. "I can't breathe!"

"Yes you can," I say.

She shakes her head, a panicked look in her eyes. But all the while she's breathing – breathing fast and raggedly, her chest heaving up and down. "No I can't, no I can't," she says, clutching her chest. "I can't breathe."

"Belle!" My sharp voice gets her attention. "Listen to me. You *are* breathing. You're doing it right now."

Tears roll down her cheeks and she nods. "Yeah, I guess I am."

I smile. "It's okay. It's going to be okay."

She shakes her head. "Sophia, it's happening again. It's happening. I can't make it stop."

"The panic?" I ask.

She nods again, her whole body shaking as tears roll down her cheeks. I've done a bit of research on panic attacks since I moved here, and I know that the people experiencing them will often think they are dying, or that they'll never be okay. But the symptoms will fade. She will be okay, and I want to help her feel that way.

"Let's sit down," I say, putting my arm around her shoulders and leading her to her bed. "Want me to call Aunt Kate?"

"No," she says harshly, like I'd just asked if she wanted me to punch a kid. "My mom doesn't need to know. She'll just worry."

"Okay."

I pat her back, hoping I'm doing this whole comforting thing right. My mom never comforted me when I was growing up, but I've had enough nannies over the years. They always patted my back when I was upset.

"What do you want to do?"

She sniffles and wipes tears from her eyes. "I just want it to stop."

"How did it stop last time?"

She shrugs. "I don't know. Time, I guess."

"What if we watch Netflix and take your mind off it?"

"Okay."

I get her computer ready and then raid her snack drawer for some candy, chips, and chocolate. We only have bottled water in here, and I want to go get a soda from the cafeteria because nothing says comfort food like sugary junk, but Belle doesn't want me to leave. So water it is.

She's still jittery and anxious for the rest of the day. She also keeps apologizing, saying she's sorry I'm skipping class for her. I tell her it's totally okay.

I'm taking care of my cousin when she needs me. Shelfbrooke can just deal with it.

AN ENTIRE WEEK goes by before Belle feels comfortable enough to let me go to class. Luckily, my aunt stepped in after the first day and plead my case in front of the administration, and they allowed me to do my school work from my dorm on a temporary basis so I can take care of Belle.

Now, it's a fresh new week, and Belle hasn't had a full blown panic attack in three days.

"You sure you're okay?" I ask for the tenth time this morning.

"Yes," she says with a nod. "I'll be okay."

"Call me if you need anything. I have a special note from Dean Thomas saying I'm allowed to leave class to come see you, so don't worry about getting me in trouble."

She nods again.

I go to leave, and she calls my name. I turn back around.

"I still want to go to the garden," she says. "Sometime soon."

The knot in my stomach tightens a bit. I haven't had any time to look for the key in the last week of being here with Belle. As much as I want to get into the hidden garden too, I can't do anything without the key.

"I don't know..." I say. "I don't want you to do too much too fast."

"Please, Sophia. I want to go."

"The last time you stepped out of this dorm, you had a massive panic attack. The gardens are a long walk away."

"I know... but if it's at night... I think I can handle it."

I give her a look. "I'm serious!" she says. "I think I'll be fine."

"We can talk about this later."

"You sound just like my mom." She folds her arms across her chest.

"Good. Because your mom only wants the best for you, and so do I."

Before she can answer, I close the door and walk

quickly down the hallway, confident that she won't follow me.

I feel awful for discouraging her from going outside again, because like it or not, Belle will never get better if she doesn't try. Baby steps and all that. But I can't just take her to the garden right now. The door is locked. If I don't find the key, I'll never be able to take her.

"Sophia!" Declan calls my name embarrassingly loud across the campus. He jogs toward me, and I'm still not sure how I feel about him. He stopped being my friend because some idiot told him not to talk to me. I mean, I get that the idiot in question is threatening his job, but still. That sucks.

"What is it?" I say, deciding to go with the cold, unfriendly approach. It's easier if you don't have feelings for someone.

"You're finally back. Where have you been? It was impossible to find you. Do you not have a Knight Watch profile?"

I snort. "No. That website is stupid."

"Is everything okay?" he asks, falling into step with me.

"Why would I answer you? We're not friends, remember?" I look over at him and see the hurt in his eyes. It feels good to know I caused that pain. He's certainly caused me enough of it.

"I'm sorry," he says. "I really am. But I'm not sure what to do. I like you, Sophia."

His voice hitches on that last bit. He swallows. "If we weren't at this stupid school, I'd be around you all the time. I'd ask you out. I'd do whatever it takes to get your attention."

My heart lodges in my throat. No one has ever talked to me like that before. "Why are you telling me this?" I say, my voice so quiet I barely hear it.

"Because it's true." Declan lets out a frustrated sigh and meets my gaze. "I really like you. But Chad Stokes could ruin my life."

"So maybe you should stay away from me," I say, swallowing the lump in my throat.

"I don't want to."

"I don't want you to, either, but I also don't want that dude ruining your life. What does he have over you, anyway?"

"It's not about me," he says, glancing around as if he's afraid someone will overhear. But the nearest students are a good two minutes ahead of us on the sidewalk. "It's about you, actually."

"What does that mean?"

He shrugs. "He hates you. Like... as much as you *can* hate someone."

"But why? I don't even know him."

A cool breeze carries the scent of Declan's cologne toward me. I look over at him, feeling the attraction grow no matter how much I don't want it to.

"He made it seem like you do."

I frown. "Do you have a picture of him?"

Declan takes out his phone and looks up Chad Stokes on Night Watch. I stare at his photo for a minute, the boring face seeming vaguely familiar the longer I look at it.

And then it hits me.

I remember.

"Oh... no..."

"What?" Declan says.

I curse under my breath. "Yeah, I know him. And I know why he hates me."

Curiosity swims in Declan's ocean blue eyes but he doesn't ask me to clarify. Maybe he's scared to.

"His dad does business in California," I explain. "He used to show up at parties when we were sixteen and try to hook up with girls, but none of my friends wanted him. He was just so...desperate. It was gross."

"He hates you because you rejected him?" Declan asks.

"Nope. He hates me because I caught him slipping a roofie into my friend's drink. He turned into a total crybaby. He swore he had never done that before and it was his first time. He apologized and cried and offered me anything I wanted to keep my mouth shut, so I lied and told him I wouldn't say anything. But then I went straight to the police and he was arrested."

"No way." Declan's eyebrows disappear underneath his hair.

I nod. "His daddy had to pay a crap ton of money to cover the whole thing up and get his record sealed. Shelfbrooke totally would have kicked him out of this school if they knew."

"Wow."

"I guess he heard I was coming here and wanted to make sure I didn't tell anyone about his shady past, but the joke is on him because I didn't even know he went here. I just wanted to get through senior year without any drama."

Declan's hand lightly brushes against mine, our fingers interlocking for a brief moment. "I'm sorry."

"You should go." I pull my hand away from his, not because I want to, but because I can't stand the idea of Chad Stokes doing anything to hurt him or his job in the gardens. "Maybe we can hang out later," I say. "Like... secretly?"

He smiles. "I'd really like that."

"Cool. And maybe you could tell me more about that necklace."

He reaches up and grabs the pendant around his neck. "What about it?"

"Is there anything else with that symbol on it?" I ask.

His eyes widen. "No," he says, a little rude. "Whatever rumor you've heard, it's not true."

"Okay, well now I'm intrigued," I say with a smile. "What rumors are we talking about?"

He eyes me suspiciously. "Have you heard one?"

"No." And it's not a lie, because I haven't *heard* anything.

He doesn't look like he believes me. "You've been reading those history books on the school. You want to know about the secret door, don't you?"

My heart stops. "Do you have the key?"

He rolls his eyes. "You're the smartest girl I know. I can't believe you're falling for these stupid lies."

"What lies?" I say. "The secret door is real."

"No, it isn't. Every few weeks, someone hears some stupid rumor and they come to me wanting the Moss family crest to be the answer to the rumors. There is no door, Sophia."

I start to object, to tell him that there is a door, that I've seen it, but we're at Kellylynch Hall now.

"Just drop it," he says softly. "There is no door. There is no key. We can be friends but not if you only want me for something that doesn't exist."

CHAPTER FIFTEEN

NOW THAT I know the key is a real thing, the garden consumes me. Declan so much as admitted it when he said there is no key. He was clearly lying. But it's hard to get more information from him because I'm trying to stay away from him.

Not because we're enemies, but because we're friends. I also did some digging on this Chad Stokes guy and he's bad news. His dad is the person who gets involved in political scandals and suddenly the politician everyone was mad at disappears. If he can do that to a high profile person, I shudder to think of what he'd do to Declan, a regular high school kid with no famous family. He could ruin his life.

So I stay away.

Declan and I exchange small smiles in class, but only

if no one is looking. Sometimes we say hello if we pass each other on campus. But every time he tries to talk to me, I say no. I whisper, "I don't want you in trouble."

It is totally my luck that the one time I did something not selfish by reporting Chad two years ago, my good deed came back to ruin my high school experience. But I can't fret over it now. All I truly care about is finding that key and getting into the garden. Even my crush on Declan takes a backseat while I obsess over trying to find it.

Two weeks pass. I sit through class each day, desperate for the bell to ring so I can walk back out to the garden and look for the key. I've started thinking that maybe the key is hidden somewhere near the garden door. If the door is hidden, then maybe the key is, too. It only makes sense.

But as the days drag on and I still haven't found anything, I start getting worried that maybe the key is hidden somewhere else. These gardens are huge. Maybe it's hanging on a hook on a wall that's been covered with decades of vine growth. It's only three months until graduation. I'll never find it at this rate.

And then I'll never get to bring Belle to the garden. She'll never start to overcome her anxieties.

It'll all be because I can't find this hidden key.

Frustrated with another day of wandering around

the garden until the sun sets, I start to make my way back to the dorm. I've been here so often that I know these pathways now. I can get to the hidden door five different ways. Even in the dark, I can make my way back without needing a flashlight.

Yet I can't find the key.

Disappointment floods through me as I slowly walk back to the dorm. It's just after seven, and I wish the sun didn't set so early so I'd have more time to search. I thought about bringing a flashlight, but I don't want to draw attention to myself. I've learned that the students don't tend to wander very far into the gardens, probably because they're afraid they'll get lost. Once I get deep enough in the maze of beautiful greenery, I don't have to worry about running into anyone. Bringing a flashlight might change that, though. I don't want to draw any attention to myself or to the hidden garden door.

I stop by the dining hall and grab dinner to go. I text Belle asking what she wants to eat, but she doesn't reply. After a few minutes of waiting around, I decide to grab her the same thing I'm getting myself, which is pasta alfredo with garlic bread and a side salad.

My hands are full as I make my way down the hallway to our dorm, so I kick at the bottom of the door with my foot instead of knocking. "Belle? It's me."

I wait a few seconds, but she doesn't answer the door. "Belle?"

Maybe she's in the shower, which would explain why she never answered my text. I set the bags of food on the floor and reach for my key. As soon as the door opens, Belle calls out my name.

"Finally!" she says. "Oh my God, it hurts so much. I'm so glad you're home."

"What's going on?" I say, rushing inside, the food forgotten on the floor. The dorm room is a mess. Belle is sprawled on the floor near her bed, hunched over her ankle. A stepladder is also on the floor, tipped sideways, as well as a container that used to hold thumbtacks. Now the thumbtacks are scattered all over the floor, like tiny little landmines.

On her bed, a strand of clear twinkly lights blink and glow, half thumb-tacked to the wall, and half dangling on the bed.

I slide my foot across the floor, clearing a pathway out of the thumbtacks so I can get to my cousin.

"Are you okay?"

She draws in a ragged breath and nods. "It's my ankle. I think it might be broken."

"Oh God." I drop to my knees and look at her foot. Her skin is pale and swollen, her ankle now the size of a softball.

"Can you move it?"

She wiggles her toes. "Kind of. It hurts really bad."

I look around. "Let me guess. You were standing on a stepladder on top of your mattress trying to hang twinkly lights on the wall?

She looks chagrined as she nods. "I just wanted them way up high, so I stood on the stepladder."

"A stepladder on a mattress is not a good idea."

"Trust me, I know that now."

She sighs and looks back at her ankle. "I've been here for about two hours. My phone is over there and I didn't have the energy to get it. I just kept waiting for you to get home."

"Belle, I'm so sorry." I sweep my arms out, trying to round up as many thumbtacks as I can. Before either one of us moves around too much, this floor needs to be cleaned.

"What'd you leave outside?" she asks.

"Oh crap, the food." I rush back and get it, grateful that I'd piled all our food containers into a plastic bag for the walk home. Sometimes I just carry them without a bag, but I'm not sure I'd want to eat food that had been on the floor without the extra layer of protection. "You hungry?"

She nods, and then winces again.

After the thumbtacks are cleaned up, I sit on the floor

with my cousin and we eat dinner. I try to examine her ankle, even though I'm nowhere near being a doctor, so I don't know what I'm looking at. The swelling is only getting worse, and now her skin is a little bruised. She's able to get up with my help, but she can't put any weight on her foot.

"Belle..." I say, as I help her sit on her bed. Tears stream down her cheeks. "I think you need a doctor."

"No, I'm fine."

I give her a look. She blinks and more tears fall from her eyes. I don't know if they're from the pain, or her fear of leaving her room. "I don't want to leave," she whispers.

"I'm calling Aunt Kate."

"No!" Belle says.

But it's too late. Her safety is at risk here, and I'm calling. I press the phone to my ear and it rings. Several moments pass and Aunt Kate doesn't answer the phone.

"We have to do something," I say. "You need a hospital. If it's broken, you'll need a cast."

She shakes her head. "Let's just hang out a few days and see what happens. I might get all better."

"Or you might get worse," I say. "Let me call an ambulance."

"No way. That's way too much attention. Everyone will see."

"Not if they drive up to our dorms. I'll ask that they keep the lights off. Maybe no one will see you. It is late, after all."

"But if they do see me, it'll be even more humiliating than if someone saw me normally. And I can't even do normally right now, Sophia."

I heave a sigh. "What if I snuck you out? Just like we've talked about. It's almost dark, anyway. We'll wait until after curfew and sneak out through the gardens, then walk to your mom's house."

Belle considers this for a long moment. "But I can't walk."

"I'll help you."

She bites her bottom lip.

"If it's broken, you need medical care," I say, hoping that sways her.

She nods. "Okay. But only after midnight."

I reluctantly agree. I try calling Aunt Kate a dozen more times, but she doesn't answer. This always happens in the evenings because she often forgets to turn her phone off silent mode when she gets back from work.

Belle and I attempt to watch a funny show while we wait for the clock to hit midnight. I can tell she's in a lot of pain, though, and I wish she'd just let me call a freaking ambulance. Or an Uber. I ask her multiple times, but the answer is always no.

Finally, it's time.

Belle dresses in a pair of loose-fitting sweatpants because it's all that will pull over her swollen ankle, and a black hoodie. I put a fuzzy sock on her bad foot and together we stand up. She wraps her arm around my shoulders and I wrap mine around her, and we shuffle out of our dorm room. We're down the hall and to the doors before Belle says anything.

"Whoa." Her eyes go wide as I try to shuffle to the side and open the door while still holding onto her. "I've been in so much pain, I barely noticed being in the hallway."

I smile. "Maybe this ankle pain is what will help you overcome your anxiety."

To my surprise, she smiles back. "Maybe."

We step outside and Belle gasps as the crisp night air hits us.

"It's beautiful," she says, gazing up at the starry night sky. "I haven't been outside in so long."

"This way," I say, turning sharply left. We have a short walk in the open and then we can duck behind a long, overgrown hedge that leads straight to the gardens. No one ever comes back here and it's the perfect place to sneak around.

Belle's tears continue to fall as we hobble our way to the hedge.

"Are you hurting really bad?" I ask.

"Yes, but that's not why I'm crying. I'm just really, really glad I'm finally outside."

I smile, but she probably can't see it in the darkness. "I'm glad, too."

We make it to the first bench on the inner edge of the gardens and then we sit down to rest. Belle can't stop looking around, even though the dim street lamps and the half-moon in the sky makes it a little hard to see. I'm keeping us on the outer rim of the gardens, which is the most popular walkway, and has the highest probability that we'll run into some other students who are also staying out past curfew, but I don't tell her that. I don't want to worry her, but there's no way we could walk into the center of the gardens. It would take too long. She needs a doctor now. Luckily, just across campus, we'll only have a short two block walk until we're at her mom's apartment complex. Then she can take us to the hospital.

"Ready?" I say, after we've rested on the bench a while. Belle nods. She stands up on her good foot and then reaches out for me.

"Tell me about the garden you're going to take me to someday. The hidden garden."

"Well, we'll have to wait until your ankle is healed first," I say. It's true, but the extra time is also needed so I can find the key. Belle doesn't know about that part yet.

"But then you'll take me to it?" she asks, her voice hopeful.

"Yeah, of course."

"So where is it?"

"It's hidden deep inside these gardens," I say as we walk along the worn path. "It takes about fifteen minutes to walk to it from here."

"Isn't this place a labyrinth?"

"Yes, but I know the way. It's hidden behind a secret door that no one else knows about."

"Then how do you know about it?"

"I found it on accident. Well... sometimes I think the bird wanted me to find it. Like maybe that little bird just knew what I needed. A secret place. Somewhere to escape this cruel world."

"I can't wait to see it."

"You will," I assure her. "All we have to do is make it there, and then go into the hidden door. It'll be beautiful. It's breathtaking. You'll love it."

"I don't think it's possible to have anxiety in a garden like that," she says.

"Do you have anxiety right now?" I ask.

"Well... yes?" she says with a chuckle. "But... it's

okay. I'm okay... I'm ... doing this," she says, struggling for words between her labored steps. "And if I can do this, then I can go to the secret garden with you. Maybe we can have lunch there. Do our homework there."

"We will," I say, feeling guilty for not revealing that none of this can happen until I find the key.

"I can't wait."

"This way." I turn us to the left where the paths change and we need to switch directions.

As we turn, I notice something in the corner of my vision. I look back and see Declan. Standing there in his gardening uniform, his dark eyes peering right at mine, having heard everything I just said about the garden he insists doesn't exist. I turn away and keep walking, hoping he doesn't say anything that will ruin Belle's night.

CHAPTER SIXTEEN

HE DOESN'T SAY ANYTHING. After we've walked for a few harrowing seconds, I glance back to see if he's still there. It's fairly dark out here and maybe I only imagined it. At least I hope so. But as I turn around to sneak a glance, I see Declan still standing there.

He gives me a questioning look. An *are you okay?* look.

I hold out a thumbs up behind Belle's back. I've told him before that I live with my cousin and that she doesn't go outside. He didn't ask for any details and I wasn't volunteering them, but I'm glad he knows to stay quiet now. One random unexpected person might send my cousin into another panic attack.

Belle doesn't talk much as we walk fifteen minutes through the gardens to the other side of the campus.

She's too busy admiring the beauty of the gardens, even when they're covered in shadows. She stops to touch a rose bloom, and then she leans forward and smells it.

"I can't wait to come back," she says whimsically. "Let's come back tomorrow."

I bite the inside of my lip. "You need to heal first."

"Why? I'm out here now."

"Because this right here is an emergency," I say, pointing at her ankle. "We'll come back in a few weeks."

"No, tomorrow."

"It's after midnight, so it's technically already tomorrow," I say. "Wish granted."

She groans. "I thought you wanted me to go to the gardens! You said it would help my anxiety."

"I do," I say, feeling like a huge jerk. She's come so far tonight, and she's in pain, and we're about to go to the hospital, which I'm sure will be horrible on her anxiety. I just can't tell her the truth right now. All I have to do is get a little more time, a few more days to search for the key.

Belle freezes at the edge of the property. Even though there's a large stone wall that closes in the Shelfbrooke campus from the outside world, there are a few wrought iron gates that bridge the two if you know where to look. This one is in the gardens, and it leads to a road that's only two blocks away from Aunt Kate. I found it a few weeks ago.

"What if someone's out here?" Belle whispers, peering through the gate at the street on the other side.

"It's late, everyone is asleep," I assure her. We step onto the sidewalk and then quickly hobble across the street. My shoulders are aching from supporting her weight, but we're almost there. I try calling Aunt Kate again, but she doesn't answer.

"Mom is going to be so mad at me," Belle says as we approach the apartments. Aunt Kate's car is parked in the spot right in front of her apartment and Belle stares at it for a moment, like it's something familiar that she hasn't seen in a while.

"She won't be mad," I say. "Stay here." I leave Belle to lean against the porch railing and I jog up the three steps to the front door. Anxiety washes over me. This is a lot like when I first showed up here, only it's different. Everything has changed since then.

I ring the doorbell a few times in a row, hoping it'll be loud enough to wake her up. A light turns on in the living room.

The door swings open.

"Oh my God!" Aunt Kate says. She dives past me, heading straight to her daughter. "What's going on?"

"I think she broke her ankle," I say.

"I didn't want an ambulance," Belle says, winces as her mom bends down to look at her ankle.

I prepare to get a lecture about how I should have called an ambulance or something, but my aunt stays calm. She grabs her keys and throws a coat on over her pajamas, and then we get into her car, Belle stretching out in the back seat.

Everyone is silent while she drives to the hospital. I suddenly feel so stupid. I'm almost eighteen. I should be smarter than this. I should have called an ambulance instead of walking my cousin that far. I could have run to Aunt Kate's house myself and then came back to get her in the car. I should have done things very differently than I have.

We pull into the parking lot at the hospital, right up front near the emergency room. "I'll go borrow a wheelchair," I say, jumping out of the car right before it rolls to a stop.

When I bring the back wheelchair for my cousin, Aunt Kate puts a hand on my shoulder. "You did the right thing," she says softly, her voice reassuring all the insecurities inside my heart. "I'm glad you were there for her."

THE ANXIETY GODS must be smiling down on us, because the emergency room is empty. No one lingers on the waiting room chairs. Only one nurse works at the triage desk, and she takes Belle back to a room quickly. My cousin's face is white and freaked out, but she's doing okay. I stay out in the waiting room to give her some privacy with her mom.

Now that it's almost one in the morning, exhaustion is setting in. I haven't been sleeping much since I spend my time before and after school in the garden, looking for the key. Not wanting to fall asleep in the waiting room, I pick up my phone and scroll through it, just to have something to do.

There's a notification from the school's document cloud site. The one Declan and I used to work on our group project together. I click the notification and see that Declan has left a comment on our paper, even though it was turned in for a grade weeks ago.

Hey... is everything okay with your cousin?

I click reply.

Her ankle is hurt. We're at the hospital now. Here's my number if you want to text me.

A few minutes later, a new number messages me.

Much better. I didn't know how else to get ahold of you since you don't use Knight Watch.

Me: *I guess it's about time we exchange numbers.*

Now we can be secret friends. Save my number as someone else's name.

Declan: *You're taking this whole thing too seriously, I want to be your friend.*

Me: *I want to be your friend too, which is why I'm staying away from you. The Stokes are bad news.*

It's wild how my heart beats a little faster when I'm talking to Declan. Even over text, it's like my brain goes haywire with how bad I'm crushing on him, even though we can never be anything more than that.

We exchange a few more random texts, and I tell him about how Belle fell and hurt herself so we went to her mom's house to get a ride. I don't tell him about her anxieties because I don't want to share her personal business like that.

He doesn't reply for a few minutes, and I almost fall asleep again. Then my phone beeps.

Declan: *It seems like the garden is important to your cousin.*

Me: *It's important to both of us. I promised I'd take her there, but I just have to find the key first.*

Declan: *She doesn't know you don't have the key?*

Me: No... *She also doesn't know I've never actually been to the hidden garden. But I'm going to find it, and I'll get her there. I made a promise and I'm keeping it.*

Declan: *What makes you think there's a hidden garden?*

Is he messing with me? Or does he really not know? How could Declan Moss, great grandson of the founder of the Shelfbrooke gardens not know about the hidden garden inside the very place he works? But the alternative—that he's lying to me—is a little hard to swallow right now. Declan is my friend. I don't want him to lie to me.

Help me find the key and I'll show you, I text back.

That sounds like you just want an excuse to hang out with me, Declan texts. Then he sends a wink face emoji.

All the seriousness is gone now. We're back to flirting and playful banter. Maybe he really doesn't know about the garden.

Believe it or not, there's more to my life than flirting with cute gardeners, I text.

Like what? He texts. *Looking for places that don't exist?*

Oh it exists. I just need to find the key.

The double doors of the emergency room open and my aunt walks out, pushing Belle in a wheelchair. I shove my phone back in my pocket and stand up.

"What did they say?"

"Not broken," Aunt Kate says. "But it's a pretty bad

sprain. She has to wear this walking boot for a few weeks and stay off it for a while."

"Well that's mostly good news," I say, looking at my cousin. Someone gave her a blue fleece hospital blanket, and she's got it wrapped around her chest like a shawl. She looks up at me and nods. "Can we please get home now."

"Of course," Aunt Kate says. "I'm not go into sneak you back into campus right now. You two can stay in Belle's room at my house and I'll take you back in the morning."

"I'm not going back to school unless it's dark outside," Belle says.

Aunt Kate gives me a look like *what are you gonna do* and then rolls her eyes. "Whatever you say, sweetheart."

We pile into her car and drive back to her apartment. Belle passes out on the short drive, thanks to the high dose of pain meds she got in the hospital. I help my aunt carry her inside and put her in bed, then I make a place to sleep on the couch. It's so late, I can barely keep my eyes open, and when I lay down in my aunt's living room, I put my phone on the coffee table, but notice there's a new text from Declan. He sent it just a few minutes after the last text I sent him.

I open it.

You mean this key? The text says. There's a photo below. I click it.

It's a silver skeleton key with the same symbol on the handle that's on the lock at the hidden door.

All these weeks I spent looking for it and it was right there the whole time.

Declan has the key.

CHAPTER SEVENTEEN

I CAN HARDLY SLEEP for the rest of the night, and it's not because I'm on a couch in a strange place. It's because Declan has the key. He has the key! It takes everything I have not to squeal out in excitement and wake up my aunt and cousin.

I have school the next morning, and after eating Aunt Kate's delicious French toast for breakfast, she drives me back to Shelfbrooke. Belle stays home with her because she doesn't want to come back to the dorms until it's dark outside and we can sneak her back inside.

There is so much going on right now with my cousin and the amazing fact that she's left her dorm for the first time in three years, but I feel selfish because all I can think about is that key. I need the key. I can't wait to get it.

And of course, because life isn't fair, I'm suck at school all day with no ability to talk to Declan. He makes eye contact with me in English class, and again in the hallways and during chemistry, but I try not to do anything other than a simple smile. You never know if one of the Big Five are watching, waiting to tattle on us to Chad Stokes.

At lunch, I eat alone in my dorm, and I imagine a world where things were different. Where Chad Stokes didn't exist, and Declan lived in Malibu. Where we could flirt and date and be together without fear of repercussions. A world where Belle didn't have anxiety and she could hang out with us outside, in the sunshine, with no worries at all.

I pick up my phone to look at the picture of the key again, and that's when I realize I forgot to text him back. Duh, Sophia! I didn't text last night because it was late and I didn't want to accidentally wake him up.

I quickly type out a reply.

You have the key! Can I please please please borrow it?

His reply is instant.

Declan: *It's just a decoration.*

Me: *No, I promise it isn't.*

Declan: *What makes you think you know more about my family's history than I do?*

***Me**: Meet me at the staff dorms tomorrow morning and I'll show you.*

It takes him a while to reply, like maybe he's thinking about it. My heart skips a beat and my hands get shaky as I sit here staring at my phone, waiting for him to reply. We can't meet up after school because I promised to go to my aunt's house to see Belle and smuggle her back into the dorms tonight after dark. But tomorrow is Saturday, and the campus is just as empty bright and early on Saturdays as it is at night.

My phone beeps.

Declan: *Okay... but only because I want to see you. Not because I believe that this key actually leads to anything.*

My heart flutters. He wants to see me. I want to see him.

But more than anything, I want to get into that garden.

Me: *Can we go early? Like 7am?*

Declan: *You think 7am is early? Gardeners get up at 5 ;-)*

I grin and text him back: *5 it is!*

BELLE DOESN'T COME HOME the first night. Aunt Kate calls and tells me she's having another panic attack and wants to stay longer. The dorm room is so quiet and weird when I'm the only person in it. I manage to fall asleep around midnight, and when my alarm goes off at four thirty in the morning, I desperately wish I could stay in my warm, comfortable bed.

But I have a garden to explore.

I get up, throw on some clothes, and spend more time than I want to admit putting on makeup and fixing my hair. I want to look cute for Declan, even though he's seen me looking pretty lame in my school uniform. Technically, we're supposed to wear our uniforms on weekends too, but it's so early, I really don't think we'll run into anyone. At least I hope not.

I slip out the door right at five, and see Declan standing outside the staff dorms, waiting for me. I can't help but grin.

"Hey," I say, walking outside to meet him. "You have the key?"

He pulls it from his pocket. The key is longer than your normal key. It's longer than the length of my hand, heavy and sturdy. He holds it out to me.

I take it gently, reverently. This key means everything to me right now and I can't believe I finally have it in my hand.

"What makes you think you'll find a secret door for this key?" Declan says as we walk toward the nearest garden hedge.

"I've already found it," I say.

He snorts. "There's no way. I know these gardens in and out."

"So you know about the secret door?"

He quirks an eyebrow. "There is no secret door."

"Clearly you don't know the gardens as well as you think you do."

He frowns. "Are you serious? Do you seriously know a secret door? Or is this some elaborate joke?"

We slip into the gardens, and I lead the way. The path to the hidden garden is intricate, with lots of twists and turns, and it takes about fifteen minutes to walk there at a normal pace. But I know it by heart.

"Of course I'm serious," I say. "Why would I be joking about this?"

He shoves his hands in his pockets. "The hidden garden is a rumor at Shelfbrooke. A legend. I don't know how it got started, but people are always passing it around from one class to the next. So naturally, everyone comes to the gardener—me—thinking I'll tell them where it is. But it doesn't exist. My dad doesn't know anything about it, and neither does my grandfather. I don't think they would lie to me, either. It's just really annoying whenever someone starts being my friend and then I realize it's because they want access to a place that doesn't exist."

"Trust me, this is real," I say. "I wouldn't lie to you."

Declan is cute when he looks skeptical. I lean over and bump into him as we walk. "I promise."

He grins. "How did you find it?"

I snort. "Oh you know...wandering around the gardens feeling sorry for myself."

"I'm sorry everyone treats you like crap. I mean, you weren't exactly super nice to me when we met but, you don't deserve that."

An ache rises up in my chest. I look over at him. "I'm sorry for how I treated you when we met."

"You've already apologized for that," he says, stopping at an intersection of the garden pathways.

"I know, but... I feel like I should say it more."

"It's fine. I promise." Declan looks left and then right. "Which way do we go?"

"This way."

We walk a little further, and as we get deeper and deeper into the gardens, Declan keeps sneaking little glances at me. Like maybe he's wondering if I'm lost. But I'm not lost.

We approach the wall with the hidden door. I stop and turn to him. "Key, please."

He hands it to me.

I take a deep breath. If this doesn't work, I'll be crushed. Belle won't have a garden to visit. I'll be a liar who let her down.

My teeth wear into my bottom lip as I approach the wall. From here it just looks like vines of green leaves that stretch wide and tall. But I know what lies underneath it. I feel for the door, and then uncover the lock. I slide the key into the hole, and it fits perfectly. I twist it.

It's rusted and old and hard to turn, like my dorm room lock was when I first moved in. But I put some muscle into it, refusing to be proven wrong. This will work. It has to.

The lock clinks, and releases.

"Holy crap," Declan breathes from beside me. I look up at him and grin. "Can you help me?"

We both grab the large metal handle and pull. The door easily opens a few inches, abut then the vines are all overgrown and blocking us. Declan takes a pair of garden sheers from his pocket and gently snips at all of the vines, until the outline of the door is visible.

The door swings open. I bounce up and down on my toes.

"I can't believe it," he says, looking down at me.

"Why don't you go first?" I say.

He holds out his hand. "Together."

I reach for it, and a jolt of electricity shoots through my body as we hold hands. We step through the door and into the hidden garden.

The area in front of us is rounded, with polished cobblestones making a circular path around a large granite fountain in the middle. Water gushes through the fountain just like it does in all of the other fountains in the rest of the gardens, only this one hasn't been touched in a very, very long time. There are roses and lilies and orchids, and dozens of flowers that I can't name, all left to grow and flourish on their own.

We see little bits of other statues around the garden, that are mostly covered up from the flowers and vines. An angel here, a small child there. One even looks like a puppy.

The air smells better than any flower bouquet I've ever had. It's a perfect mixture of floral and sunshine, and I wish I could wear it as a perfume.

Declan and I wander around in silence for a few minutes, just taking in the sight of the beauty around us. There is only one bench in here, a large wooden masterpiece that's set up like a throne that's big enough for two people to sit on.

I run my hand across the wood and then look up at Declan.

"This is the most beautiful thing I've ever seen."

He takes a step forward, his silky hair glistening in the sunlight, his eyes sparkling from the water in the fountain. “It’s the second most beautiful thing I’ve ever seen,” he says softly.

He’s close enough now that I can see the little dots of gold in his eyes.

“What could be more beautiful than this?” I ask, my breath hitching when he reaches forward and touches my cheek.

“You.”

I try to smile, but I’m so nervous that it probably comes out looking weird. It doesn’t matter though, because one breath later, my smile is covered with Declan’s kiss. His lips are soft, but his arms are strong as they wrap around me.

I relax against him, and kiss him back. And every bad thing that has happened up until now suddenly feels like it was all worth it.

CHAPTER EIGHTEEN

DESPITE OVERCOMING her trip to the hospital, Belle doesn't want to leave her mom's house for the next few days. As much as I want her back so I can show her the garden, I'm also enjoying my secret meetings with Declan in the times we can get away. Every day after school, we bring our homework and some snacks to the garden and hang out like a real couple. We take different routes so no one sees us walking together. Declan brings his gardening tools and he teaches me how to prune and tend to the flowers that have overgrown from their planters. Together, we work hard every day, bringing the garden back to its original beauty. I never knew I'd like a hobby like gardening, but it turns out I love it.

We still don't know who made this garden, or why, but we figure it was probably one of Declan's ancestors since the key has the same symbol as his necklace, which was passed down from his dad.

This garden is our own paradise. After a week of diligent work, we've made it into something spectacular. Here, we can be friends. We can be more than friends. We can flirt, and laugh, and even kiss.

And we definitely kiss.

But it's more than that. This garden is my favorite place in the world. And I can't wait to bring Belle here.

One day after school, Declan tells me he'll be late to the garden because he's going out to dinner with his family for his mom's birthday. I use the time to walk to Aunt Kate's apartment and visit Belle.

"The garden is so beautiful," I tell her as we share a banana split made from all four of the ice cream flavors in Aunt Kate's freezer. "You're going to love it so much."

"Are you sure it's hidden?" Belle says. Her long brown hair is twisted into two French braids, and it looks really cute on her. I want to ask her to braid my hair soon.

"It's totally hidden," I say, scooping a bite of chocolate ice cream. "Only Declan and I know about it."

"Wait a minute," she says, pointing her spoon at me. "Why'd you say it like that?"

"Say what?"

Her eyes go wide. "You like Declan!"

The blush in my cheeks tells her all she needs to know. Her jaw drops. "I can't believe it! You fell for a Shelfbrooke boy!"

"Shut up," I whisper, hoping Aunt Kate doesn't overhear. I don't know why the thought of talking about boys with my aunt is embarrassing, but it is. "We're just friends."

"Friends who kiss each other?" Belle asks, wiggling her eyebrows.

I bite my lip. "Maybe."

"Oh. My. God!" Belle slides closer to me on the couch. "Tell me everything."

"I'll tell you in the garden," I say. "Whenever you want to go."

She pouts and then sits up straighter. "Okay. I need to do this. I want to do this." She glances back at the kitchen, where her mom is washing dishes. "Maybe even tonight."

I clap my hands together. "Yay! You are going to love the garden. It's amazing."

Belle's grin is so genuine, I can't even see the traces of anxiety that usually linger in her eyes. "I can't wait."

After eating way too much ice cream, I walk back to Shelfbrooke and stop by the gardens. Declan will probably be back from his family dinner soon, so I'll just wait in the beautiful evening weather until he gets to our secret meeting place.

I can't believe how much things have changed since I started at this school back in January. I'm a better person now. I'm not stuck on social media or the Malibu party life. I don't have fake friends who don't actually care about me. I'm doing well in school, and although no one talks to me during class, it doesn't matter, because I have Declan and Belle, and they're genuine friends.

There are only two months until school ends, and then we'll start on the next adventure. Declan and I haven't talked about graduation yet. I don't really want to. I'm afraid he's going to stay here and I'm going to leave and we'll never see each other again. But life is unpredictable, life is fun. And life can be changed. Whatever happens, I have to put my all into it and hope that it will work out.

I'm lying on a blanket that I brought from my dorm when my phone rings. It's my mom. She hasn't reached out to me in weeks.

"Hello?" I say, tilting my head up to the evening sun.

"Good news," she says. "You get to leave Shelfbrooke."

I sit up. "What?"

"Your father and I are moving to Africa for the next

two years. It's for some charity thing we agreed to host. The benefits will be huge."

I know more than anyone that the charity work my parents do is usually some thinly veiled opportunity to get even richer while sending one or two percent of their funds to the actual charity. "What does that have to do with me?"

"You're coming along, dear. We'll hire the best tutors for you."

"But I only have two months left here. It would be easier just to stay."

"I thought you hated that school!" Mom says in her typical haughty voice. "All you did was complain and complain and now you want to stay? What's wrong with you, Sophia?"

"I made friends. I like living with Belle. And I'm almost done anyway," I say. "Pulling me out of school now is just stupid."

"What's stupid would be turning down the opportunity to secure a wealthy man as a husband before you're too old to be wanted anymore."

My jaw drops. "What are *you* smoking, Mom?"

I'll be eighteen in a week. It's not like I've reached spinster age yet.

"You won't be young and beautiful forever, Sophia. There are many amazing families staying in

Africa this summer and I want you to meet them all."

"So I'll visit in the summer," I say. "I'm not leaving school until I graduate."

"You need to go now, honey. You cannot pass up the opportunities to meet these worthy young men before they head off to college."

"Worthy. You mean rich? I don't care about getting a rich boyfriend, Mom."

My mom laughs. "Oh, Sophia. You can be funny when you want to."

"It's not a joke. And I'm not going to Africa."

I hang up the phone.

Mom doesn't call me back.

I'm still fuming mad when the hidden door opens up a few minutes later. Declan enters into our secret hideaway dressed in dark jeans and a blue button up shirt. He looks good. He looks handsome.

"Hey," he says, smiling in that shy but adorable way he smiles when we see each other.

I get up and walk over to him. "Thank you for being one of the three decent people in my life."

He quirks an eyebrow. "Um... you're welcome?"

I laugh and throw my arms around his neck. "Kiss me," I say.

He grins and pulls me close. "Yes ma'am."

CHAPTER NINETEEN

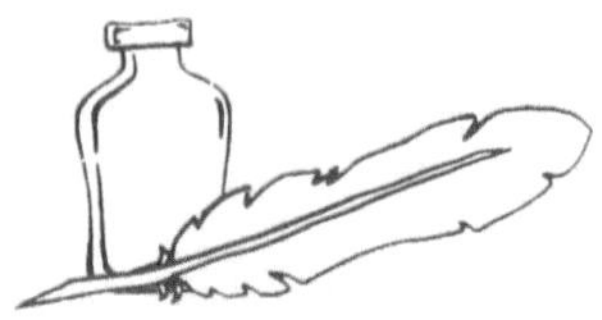

DECLAN'S KISSES ARE SWEET. Full of meaning. Desire. They're also a little timid, a little scared. Like we're both teetering on the edge of something real, and we can feel it, but we know it won't last. He's from the east coast, I'm from the west coast. It's a classic tale of two lovers who just can't be together.

But maybe I don't want that to be our ending. Maybe there's more to life than accepting the inevitable.

"Declan?" I pull away, my arms sliding down from his shoulders until my palms press against this chest.

He reaches up and grabs my wrist, his gaze a little hazy from kissing. "Yes?"

"Can we talk a minute?"

"Of course." He answers too quickly. He doesn't fully understand what I'm asking.

I shake my head and take a step back. Take a deep breath. "I want to talk to you, like for real. Not just fun easy stuff. I want to tell you the total crap going on in my life right now."

"Okay..." he says, his head tilting to the side. "You can just tell me anything, Sophia. You don't have to ask first, or like, warn me or whatever."

"It's kind of a big deal, though. I don't normally share my feelings, and all that stuff."

Declan smiles, this cute grin that makes my knees weak. "I guess I believe that. You are a little stone cold sometimes."

"Yeah. I have to be. It's how I was raised. And well... you're not just some trust fund kid at a party that I'll never see again."

"I'm not a trust fund kid at all," he says.

"No, you're not. You're real. You're kind. I like you, Declan."

"I like you, too."

I grin. And then all the problems in my life come slamming back into my subconscious, only momentarily blotted out by Declan's adorable smile. I can't get rid of them forever. My problems are too big for that.

I heave a sigh and sit on the bench, patting the place next to me for Declan to sit. "My mom called. She wants to pull me from school."

"This close to graduating?" he says, sounding incredulous. Like he thinks that maybe I'm playing a stupid joke on him.

"Yep," I say, my voice dry of any emotion. "She and my dad are moving to Africa for a while and she wants me there, too. I told her I'm not going, but... my mom always gets her way."

"Wow... that's... that's not good."

"I know." I reach over and put my hand on top of his. "I don't want to leave Shelfbrooke. Well... maybe I *can* leave Shelfbrooke," I say with a chuckle. "But I don't want to leave you. Or Belle. Or even my Aunt Kate. I like it here. I like being around you guys. And even if I go with my parents for a year or two, how will I find you again? You and Belle will have moved on to college and have all new lives."

"You would have a new life too," he says, staring at the ground. "I guess we just weren't meant to be."

"No... don't say that."

"It's true, though."

My fingers close over his. My teeth dig into my bottom lip. "I hate this. I don't want to go."

"When are you leaving?"

"I don't know. I hung up on her."

"Well, let's make the most of the time we do have," he says softly. His fingertips are rough, calloused from hours spent tending to this very garden, but I love the feel of them on my cheek. He tips my head up until my eyes lock on his, and then he presses his lips to my forehead.

"Come here."

I slide over closer to him, and he wraps his arms around me. I fit so perfectly against his chest, and it's hard to imagine my life going on without having Declan next to me. I hate my parents for doing this to me. I shouldn't be hauled around to wherever they want me to go, looking pretty like their perfect daughter. I am far from perfect. I arrived here as a spoiled brat who took everything for granted. Now the only thing I care about is right here at this stupid school.

And I'll have to leave it.

We sit like this for a long time. Until the sun dips below the garden walls and blankets the sky in shades of gold and amber. Then my phone rings.

I reach for it, seeing Belle's number on the screen.

"Hello?"

"I'm ready to come home."

"Tonight?"

"Yeah. Is that okay with you?"

"Of course," I say, turning to look at Declan. He smiles at me. I smile back. "How are we going to do this?"

"I'm thinking midnight. Mom will take me to the garden's gate entrance across from her apartment. You meet me there, and we'll slip into the gardens again."

"That sounds great. I'll meet you at midnight."

"Sophia?" Belle asks just before we hang up. "Do you think you could take me to your hidden garden too?"

"You want to see the garden tonight?" I say, glancing up at Declan. I look around at the beauty that surrounds us. "I don't think it'll be as breathtaking if it's at night. It'll be too dark."

"I just... I'm afraid I'll get back to my dorm and be too scared to leave it again."

"Then we'll go tonight," I say.

I can hear Belle's smile through her voice. "You're the best."

"That was my cousin," I say to Declan after getting off the phone.

"I figured," he says. "Is she coming back home tonight?"

I nod.

"And she wants to see this garden?"

I nod again. "I promised I would take her one day but going at night just doesn't seem worth it."

"I'm sure it'll still be great." Declan looks up at the sky. "Maybe you'll get lucky and it'll be a full moon. It'll light up the area better."

"Maybe I'll just bring a flashlight? I don't think the light would get through these thick walls."

Declan considers this for a moment. "True."

He stands and reaches for my hand. "Let's get you home."

"What? Why! It's only eight," I protest, sticking out my tongue.

"Yeah, but you should get a little sleep before your midnight excursion."

That reminds me of the last time I was out here in the middle of the night. "Declan?" I say as we walk back out of the hidden door, locking it behind us. He hands me the key. "What were you doing out here that time I was taking Belle to her mom's and I saw you in the middle of the night?"

He shrugs. "The gardens are my favorite place. I come out here a lot."

"But in the middle of the night?"

He squints at a rose bush and then kneels down and plucks off a few bad leaves. Then he shrugs again. "Sometimes I can't sleep. I come out here and think about girls."

"Girls," I say, feeling my chest tighten.

His arm slides around my back. "Well... if I'm being honest, it was one girl."

"One girl?"

He grins and squeezes me close. "The only girl that matters."

AUNT KATE STARES INTENTLY at me as she and my cousin quickly cross over the street and meet me at the garden gate. Her brow is furrowed and little worry lines crease her face. Belle is carrying two backpacks full of the stuff I had brought her from our dorm while she was staying at her mom's house. Now it's time to bring it all back to Shelfbrooke.

"What's wrong?" I ask because my aunt looks like she's about to crumble into little pieces of anxiety.

"Nothing, nothing," she says, plastering on a fake smile. "Belle, honey, are you okay?"

"Yes, Mom," Belle says, and it's too dark to see her eyes but I'll bet she rolls them. "I feel okay. My pulse is fine and my breathing is fine. I'm okay."

Aunt Kate squeezes her into a tight hug and then releases her to me. I stand here, holding open the gate, because I'm pretty sure it's one of those fancy security gates that lock once you step out of them and keeps all the people on the non-campus side of the garden out.

"Be careful," Aunt Kate says, waving at us as we retreat into the garden.

The gate clicks closed, and Belle walks quickly away. "My mom can be so annoying," she says after we're out of earshot. "She treats me like a baby."

"She's just looking out for you," I say, leading the way through the mostly dark garden paths. "Sometimes I don't know how your mom and my mom are sisters. They are so completely different."

"Your mom is glamorous, and mine is plain," Belle says.

We turn a corner and cut through a little section of daisies that I've recently discovered is a short cut. "Your mom is nice, and my mom is also a huge B."

"Oh no. What happened?"

"I don't want to talk about it right now. This is a good night because you're out and you don't have anxiety and things are good. Let's not ruin that with talk of my mother."

"Wow, it must be really bad," Belle says.

"You have no idea," I mutter under my breath.

"New subject." Belle's voice is chirpy and I know who she's about to mention before she says it. "Anything new with Declan?"

I draw in a breath. "Yep."

"Ooh! Yay!" Belle skips ahead of me a few steps, then turns around, walking backward, her eyes radiant under the moonlight. "Tell me!"

"I will in a minute," I say, feeling ten kinds of embarrassed. But I don't know why I feel that way, because liking Declan isn't embarrassing. It's the greatest thing ever. I guess it just feels weird talking about a boy I like, who likes me back, who isn't some jerk deep down. I'm not used to it.

Belle groans. "Why in a minute? Why not now?"

"Because," I say, running my hand along the vine-covered wall. "We're here."

Belle stands in reverent silence as I retrieve the key from the pocket of my hoody. I put it in the lock and twist, then just before I open the door, I turn to my cousin. "I just have to warn you, this won't be as beautiful as it is in the daytime..."

"That's okay," she says, bouncing on her toes. "I want to see the magic garden."

"It's not magic," I say with a laugh. "It's just beautiful and secret."

I pull open the heavy door, and my jaw drops at the sight before us.

"Whoa," Belle says, taking a step forward into the garden.

I follow behind her, confused and overwhelmed and on the verge of tears, because what's in front of me is not how I left the garden earlier today. It's been transformed. In the dark of midnight, our little private oasis has been given light. All over, little battery powered fairy lights are decorating the garden. They hang from the walls, and drape across the vines. They're wrapped around the statues and fountains and they outline the wooden bench.

"You didn't tell me it had lights," Belle says, her face childlike as she gazes around at the beauty all around us.

"It didn't," I croak out. Okay, I might actually cry. This is stunning. It's beyond beautiful. It's so much better than in the daylight. "Declan must have done this. He knew I was bringing you here tonight."

"Wow, that boy is a keeper," she says, beaming at me. She takes off, skipping around the cobblestone pathway, her fingers trailing along the flowers and plants as she goes. She throws her arms out and turns in a circle. "This is amazing. This was worth leaving my dorm room. Hey, what's that?"

She points to the bench, at something I haven't noticed yet. It's a vase filled with flowers, and a little card attached to it. I open it up.

Dear Sophia and Belle,

I thought you could bring a little bit of the garden home with you. Hope you're both having a magical night.

-Declan

"Um, wow," Belle says, waving the card at me. "This boy is so totally a keeper."

I grin, because that's about all I can do right now. He must have spent hours decorating the garden tonight. No wonder he told me to go home early and get some sleep—he wanted to surprise us. And these flowers picked and arranged into a vase is some top-notch romance stuff. Totally hit it out of the park, this one. That's going to make it even harder to leave him, to leave this garden, to leave everything behind.

A single tear rolls down my cheek.

CHAPTER TWENTY

MY PHONE HAS BEEN ALMOST COMATOSE since I moved to Shelfbrooke Academy. Viv stopped calling altogether, and my other friends couldn't even spare me a text or a Snapchat now that I'm no longer in Malibu, hooking them up with party invites. But it all changes a few days later when I wake up to my phone buzzing on the nightstand.

It's not just buzzing, it's practically losing its mind.

I sit up in bed and check my phone. All the noise wakes up Belle, who puts her pillow on top of her head and rolls over.

Texts. Snaps. Even a few missed Facetime calls from friends I haven't talked to in weeks. Suddenly everyone wants to talk to me.

It takes me a few minutes, two cups of coffee, and

one trip down to the dining hall for breakfast to figure out what it's all about. My mother has decided to reveal her Africa trip to her many adoring fans, via a quick guest appearance on her favorite morning TV show. I find the clip online, and watch my mom, all dolled up and looking half her age, as she tells the hosts that she and my dad are so very happy to be making a difference with this new charity project. Then the tells them that her daughter—me—was so *thrilled* at the opportunity to help the less fortunate, that I begged to be taken out of school early so that I can come along and help.

Oh, please.

I can't believe my mom thinks she can trick me like that. Of course I have nothing wrong with helping people, but this charity isn't some praiseworthy thing. It's money laundering or tax evasion or some other fancy term for making my parents and all their rich friends even richer all under the shadow of pretending to do good in the world.

The messages from my friends are all a mixture of excited for me, jealous, or that fake kind of happy where I can tell they're glad I'll be gone longer and they can rule the party scene without me. But I don't care. I don't reply back to anyone. My life is here, in Shelfbrooke, with Belle and Declan who are my real friends.

I ignore all of it and I hang out in the dorm with my cousin.

"Soph," Belle says, her mouth full of cheese Danish, "I think I'm ready to go back."

"To the garden?"

She nods, then takes another bite. "I've been dreaming about that place. Every single night since we went."

Me too. But probably not for the same reason Belle dreams about. I can't stop thinking about that night because that night was the most romantic thing anyone has ever done for me. Declan went out of his way. He went above and beyond. Just because he wanted to, because he likes me. No guy has ever done that before. I've always felt disposable to everyone. Even to my own parents. But not to Declan.

No friend, no family member, no person on earth has ever done something like that for me.

I bite the inside of my lip to keep from grinning like a fool. I've been trying to balance my time equally between hanging out with Belle and cuddling with Declan in the garden. Both of these people are so important to me, and both of them feel like secret friends. Declan and I can't be seen in public, and Belle never goes in public.

"Okay," I say. "I'll go first and turn on the lights and

then come back and get you. What time are you thinking? Midnight?"

She shakes her head. "I want to go in the daytime."

A million reasons to tell her no cross my mind. It's too much, it's too scary, you'll freak out. But I hold them back. Belle needs me and I'm going to be there for her. So I grin.

"Sounds good to me."

We spend the next two days practicing. Once before I go to school in the morning, and several times once I get back in the afternoon. Belle has me step into the hallway first, and make sure it's clear. Then she walks to the door, takes one step out, looks around, and goes back into our dorm.

But now, after dozens of tries, she's walked all the way down the hall to the exit door with me. I step outside and peer around. A few students are on campus, but no one walks directly this way since students don't have any reason to go to the staff dorms. So no one is that close to us.

"Want to step outside?" I ask.

Her teeth dig into her bottom lip, but she nods. She's still wearing the walking boot on her sprained ankle, so her steps are slow, but she presses on, and soon she's outside. In the sunshine.

"You did it," I say, beaming at her.

My phone rings.

"Answer it," Belle says, her hand on the door of the building, but her gaze sweeping around us. "I'm okay."

I take my phone from my back pocket and check the caller ID. "It's just Declan. I'll call him back later."

"No you should answer it." Belle is the biggest supporter of my secret thing with Declan. She makes me tell her every single detail about every time I see him. She loves that we meet in the garden when we can't meet in real life. It's some kind of romantic secret like in the books she reads.

"Tell him to come over," she says.

The phone is still ringing in my hand. "Are you sure?"

She nods. "We'll order pizza for dinner."

I answer the call, and Declan is just as surprised as I am when I tell him to come visit us. I give him directions to our room, and promise him that no other students will be here. No one will see him and me together and report it back to Chad.

A short while later, I am so nervous I could burst into electricity at any moment. Belle plays music on her laptop and she braids my hair and I add a little bit of makeup to my bare face.

The pizza is ordered. All we're missing is the boy.

And then there's a knock on the door. Belle draws in a deep breath.

"You okay?" I say.

She nods. "Yes. Totally okay."

It doesn't look like she's lying, so I walk over and let Declan inside. He's more adorable than ever in jeans and a T-shirt. I usually see him in his school uniform in classes, or wearing his gardener jumpsuit while he's working. But Declan in normal clothes is a sight to see.

"You look pretty," he says softly. I know we both want to kiss, but we're also smart enough not to flash around the PDA in front of my cousin.

"Hi," Belle says with a smile. She's sitting on the foot of her bed with her sprained ankle propped up on some pillows.

"Declan, this is my cousin, Belle."

"Nice to officially meet you," he says.

I was worried this might be awkward, but Declan and Belle get along great. We talk about the garden, and how we're going to visit it soon, in the daylight.

"Spring Break is in a few days," Declan says, reaching for another slice of pizza. "Maybe we could plan a picnic or something. The Wi-Fi signal is good out there in the gardens, so we could bring a computer and watch movies."

"It'll be a mini vacation," Belle says, her eyes lighting

up. "I think I'll spend every single day of Spring Break in that garden.

I raise my glass of soda to hers in a toast. "Sounds like a plan to me."

We all press our drinks together in a celebration, and I try really hard to hold back my worries. My mom had said she was pulling me from school soon. I might not last until Spring Break.

CHAPTER TWENTY-ONE

A WOMAN WALKS into my history class and says something to my teacher in hushed tones. The teacher nods and then her eyes go straight to me. My heart races. I hope that maybe I'm just mistaken and she's looking at the person behind me.

"Sophia?" my teacher says.

Dang.

"Yes, ma'am?"

"You're needed in the office."

I grit my teeth and pack up my school work, ignoring the stares of other students in the class. I have a pretty good idea of why I'm being called to the office, and I refuse to cry in front of all these people.

But I know the tears will come sooner or later because I can't help it. My mom is here. I just know she is. She's here and she's taking me out of school. I've been ignoring her calls for two days now, and I even ignored a call from my dad, who only calls me when my mom is really mad at me.

I had stupidly thought that maybe I'd get to stay at school if she couldn't reach me. But I guess not.

My throat is tight, and my vision is blurry with unshed tears as I make my way down Kellylynch Hall. I walk slowly, taking in the sight of everything, because this is probably my last time to step foot in this building. I wonder if she's already packed up my dorm room. If she's freaked out Belle by barging in there and grabbing all my stuff.

Anger rolls through me. I stop on the second floor landing and grab my phone. I text Belle.

Me: *Everything okay?*

Belle: *Yeah, why?*

Me: *Just wondering.*

Okay good, Mom hasn't gone there and terrorized my half of the dorm. She's probably going to make me do that.

My feet feel like heavy anchors as I walk across campus toward the front office. I don't want to do this, but I have to. When I reach the doors, the same ones I walked through on my first day here, I am so angry and upset that I can barely control my breathing.

My mom isn't here. Ms. Beverly sits at the front desk. She looks up when I enter and gives me a quick smile. "Sophia Brass?"

I nod.

"There's a phone call for you." She nods to the phone on her desk.

I pick up the receiver. "Hello?"

"Sophia Elaine Brass!"

Well, she might not be here in person, but hearing her voice on the phone makes me cringe just the same. "Is your cell phone broken? Is your email broken? I have been calling all day."

I know she has. I've ignored them all. But I try for a more diplomatic answer. "Er… I'm in class. I can't answer my phone in class. School rules are different than homeschooling." I throw in that last part just to remind her that me being here is her fault.

She huffs. "I am your mother. When I call, you will answer, do you understand me?"

"Yes," I say, biting off the word even though I'd rather say a lot more. "Why are you calling?"

"I'm sending a car to get you tomorrow morning. Have your things packed. Eight a.m. sharp."

"I don't want to leave. I want to stay here and graduate."

Ms. Bev gets up and walks into another room, and I

get the distinct feeling it's to give me some privacy. I'm grateful for it. "Mom, just let me stay," I plead into the phone.

"I don't understand why you have to be so difficult. Just pack up your things and be ready to go tomorrow."

"Please, Mom. Just let me stay. I promise I'll fly to Africa as soon as I graduate."

Mom breathes a long, annoyed sigh into the phone. "You'll be eighteen in a few days," she says, sounding utterly exhausted. "Almost an adult and you still act like a child."

She hangs up the phone after reciting to me once more that she'll have a car here at eight in the morning. But I barely hear the words she's saying, because she's just given me an idea.

I've been so busy with my new life that I totally forgot about my upcoming birthday. I'll be eighteen. A legal adult.

And legal adults can't be forced to quit school, or move away, or do anything by their parents.

I just need to stay at Shelfbrooke long enough to turn eighteen.

CHAPTER TWENTY-TWO

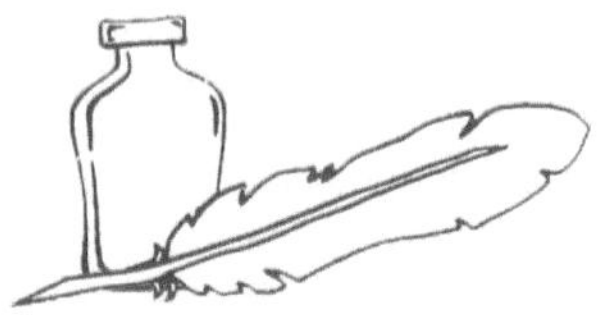

I DON'T BOTHER GOING BACK to class. There are still three classes left until the end of the day, but I have other plans to worry about now. Like how I can somehow stay at Shelfbrooke until my birthday, where I'll get to tell my parents that they can't force me to go anywhere. My tuition is all paid up anyway, and they couldn't get a refund even if I did leave now. The only smart choice is to stay and graduate.

And then maybe I can figure out another path for my life, one that isn't guided by my parents and their greedy intentions. Maybe I can do something for myself, something that makes me happy and keeps me around the people I like.

Suddenly I have a whole new understanding of my Aunt Kate. She left home when she turned eighteen, too.

She didn't want her trust fund, or the family money. She made a new life for herself here on the east coast.

Who says I can't do the same thing?

Belle is paler than usual when I get back to our dorm. "You're leaving," she says just before she crushes me to her in a hug. "I can't believe they're making you go."

"What makes you say that?"

"My mom just called. She said your mom is coming to get you tomorrow. She wanted me to be prepared for when the driver showed up in case they knocked on the door."

"Yeah, well that's not happening."

I walk past her and reach into the closet, taking out my suitcase and hefting it onto the bed. I start putting clothes in there. Enough for four days.

"Then why are you packing up?" Belle says, eyeing me like I'm not making any sense.

I turn to her. "What if when they come to get me, I'm not here?"

Belle lifts an eyebrow. "What do you mean?"

"What if I'm gone? What if they can't find me?"

"Okay..." she says, staring at me like I've lost my mind. "Are you just going to run away?"

I nod. Her eyes get even bigger. "Sophia! You can't run away! It's not safe out there."

"I'm not going far. I'm going to the garden." I give her a wild grin and then turn back to my suitcase, tossing in a few outfits, but mostly filling the space with blankets and pillows. I flip the suitcase lid closed and press down on it, zipping it up. "Just until I'm eighteen."

Belle glances at the dry erase board calendar on the wall, where I've written my birthday, which happens to fall in the middle of spring break. "That's four days from now."

I nod. "I'm going to hide out in the garden and wait until I'm old enough to make my own decisions. My parents can't take me from Shelfbrooke. I'm going to stay, and I'm going to graduate right next to you.

She puts a hand on her hip. "That's assuming I actually go to graduation. Which means I'd have to actually get over my fears long enough to attend a huge, packed ceremony."

"You will," I say. "I have faith in you."

Belle stares at me for a long time, her thoughts clearly going in circles as she thinks about my totally insane plan. She gnaws on the inside of her lip. "If you're not here when they come to get you, they'll be barging in our dorm looking for you."

"I know," I say. "And I'm sorry. Maybe you could stay with your mom for a few days? Just lie and say you have no idea where I am."

She shakes her head. "No. If you're hiding out in the garden, then I will, too."

"What?" I say, bursting out into a laugh. I don't know why this is funny, but the idea of Belle and I in the garden for four days is kind of hilarious. "You're going to be so bored! There's not even a bathroom!"

"What's your plan for that?" she says.

"I was going to slip out of the side gate, then run to your aunt's house."

She laughs. "Sounds like you've got this all figured out. I'll get my suitcase."

DECLAN CALLS me about two seconds after school gets out for the day. Belle and I have already discussed if we should tell him about our plan or not, and we've decided that's a definite yes. Declan can be trusted. And we figure someone needs to know where we're hiding just in case a freak hurricane or something comes our way.

"Hello?" I say, feeling that whoosh of warm fuzzy feelings when I answer the phone. It happens to me every time he calls or texts. Boys are weird that way.

"Are you okay? You weren't in last period. Just making sure you're not sick or something."

"I'm not sick, but... some weird stuff has happened since you last talked to me."

"Oh yeah?"

Declan's voice is so cute over the phone. "Yeah," I say, glancing at Belle. "You should probably stop by my dorm so I can tell you about it."

When he gets here, I make him sit at my desk while I tell him, because this seems like something you should be sitting down to hear. Belle stands next to me, nodding along as I talk.

"So... what do you think?" I say after revealing my plan.

"Where are you going to sleep?"

I shrug. "On the ground, I guess. We're bringing blankets."

Declan shakes his head. "No, that won't work."

Fear rockets through me. Is he going to forbid me to stay here? He's the head gardener, after all. He could rat me out in a heartbeat. "Declan, please," I start, but he holds up his hand.

"You're not sleeping on the ground. I have a tent in my dorm. I used to be in the camping club."

I crinkle my nose. "There's a camping club?"

He laughs. "Not anymore. Turns out the Shelf-brooke elite don't really care for sleeping in tents out in the wilderness. But I still have all my camping gear in my dorm. I have a tent, some solar powered lights, and a camp stove. I'll bring it to the garden."

"So you're okay with this?" I ask, peering at him as if I could somehow tell if he's lying.

Declan nods. "Let's see... I either let my girlfriend get taken away to another continent against her will, or I help her stay here with me." He lifts his hands, palms up as if weighing the options. "It's a pretty easy choice, Sophia."

"Did you just call her your girlfriend?" Belle squeals.

Declan's dark blue eyes widen. "I guess I did?"

I walk forward and wrap my arms around him. "Thank you."

"Wait," Belle says. "Are you thanking him for the girlfriend comment, or for helping us out?"

"Um... both?" I feel my cheeks blush, and then look over at Declan and his cheeks are also turning pink. We both grin at each other like idiots, and Belle makes a fake gagging sound. I don't care. Let her make fun of us. Right now I'm happy and I'm going to hold onto that feeling for as long as I can. My day started out with a terrifying trip to the office and it's ending with a gorgeous, caring boyfriend, and a plan to take my life back into my own hands.

"Okay so..." Declan stands and presses his hands

together. "I'll go get the camping gear and set it up in the garden. Do you want to meet me there later? Say, after dinner?"

"And a shower," Belle says. "Dinner and a shower and one final goodbye to my dear, precious, central air conditioning."

"I have solar powered fans," Declan says.

Belle cringes. "That is so not the same!"

I reach up and hug Declan—my new boyfriend—and then place a soft kiss on his cheek. "Thank you," I say softly.

He winks. "Anything for you."

Once he's gone, and Belle has locked the door behind him, she turns to me and says,

"This is crazy, you know that right?"

I shrug. "So what? Life is full of crazy things. But at least I get to choose this one."

CHAPTER TWENTY-THREE

IT'S THE SECOND DAY.

Belle and I have settled in nicely at our little garden retreat, which is what we've been calling it. We have pillows and tons of blankets and Declan's awesome tent which we've decorated with fairy lights. In the day time, we tend to the garden and read books and hang out under the beautiful spring sky. We have an ice chest full of snacks and drinks and Declan sneaks us meals from the dining hall. Last night wasn't nearly as weird as I'd thought it would be. The gardens are peaceful in the quiet, chilly air. And no one can find us in this hidden garden, so there was nothing to be afraid of. Belle and I had talked about my plans for when this is all over. Graduating Shelfbrooke, and going to college, and maybe sticking around here with her and my aunt. It all seems like so many decisions to make a once. Right now I just want to get through these few days until my birthday.

When the car arrived to pick me up yesterday and I wasn't there, nothing much happened for a while. I had been anxiously waiting for something, but I guess the driver only stayed a few minutes and then left when I didn't show up. It wasn't until today—a whole day later—that my mom must have realized I never got on my flight, and she's called me three times.

My phone rings again.

"You should probably answer it," Belle says. She has a pile of pink flowers at her feet and she's tying them into a flower crown. "Just get it over with."

I sigh and answer the phone. "Hi, Mom."

"Sophia! Where are you?" Wow, she actually sounds... concerned? Worried?

"I'm fine. I'm at school."

"What happened? Why aren't you here?"

"I told you I'm not going. I'm staying in school and graduating."

"You are absolutely not. I will come there and drag you out of your dorm kicking and screaming if that's what it takes."

"No offense, Mom, but I'd love to see you try."

My mom is silent for a very long time. I almost ask if

she's still there, but then she draws in a breath. "Why are you being so difficult?"

"It's not difficult, Mom. It's very, very simple. You made me enroll at a school and I'm here and I'm staying. I'm going to finish what I started, and then I'm going to run my life the way I want to."

"You better think twice about what you just said," Mom snaps. "What you are threatening is very serious."

"It is serious," I say with a nod. "It's my future. And I'm choosing to live it the way I want to."

"Your future won't be very fun if I take back your trust fund."

There it is. The ultimate threat. The one thing that keeps all my friends in line back in Malibu when it comes to their parents. They always stray, always get in trouble, but the threat of losing it all will bring them back home in a split second. This time, however, I don't think it's going to work for me. I think of my aunt, and of a life I could make for myself based off happiness, not money.

"I don't need a trust fund, Mom."

"You think you mean that but you don't," Mom says, not sounding the least bit concerned, which only makes me more set in my decision. "You have forty-eight hours to get on a plane or your trust fund is gone."

"No," I say, feeling more confident even in all the

uncertainty that lies in my future. "I have forty-eight hours until I'm a legal adult."

Mom hangs up the phone.

My heart is racing, and I'm a teensy bit freaked out, but I'm also proud of myself. I'm standing my guard. I'm doing what's right. Deep down in my heart I know if I don't stand up to my parents now, I'll end up letting them control me forever.

"What happened?" Belle asks.

I tell her everything. She watches in fascination, her jaw hanging open the whole time. "You're really just going to give up everything?"

I shrug. "Money isn't everything."

She smiles. "My mom will be proud of you."

"That's good, because she's probably the only family member who will come to my graduation."

Aunt Kate must have some kind of mind reading capabilities, because Belle's phone rings, her mom's picture appearing on the screen. "Hello?" she says.

I can hear Aunt Kate frantically talking on the other end of the line. She asks where we are, where Belle is, and then where I am all at the same time. I guess she doesn't realize that's just three different ways to ask the same question.

"We're fine," Belle says. She puts the phone on speaker, and I also try to reassure her that we're fine. She says my mom is livid and has sent Charlie down to find me, only to realize my dorm is empty. The administration doesn't know where I am because I haven't signed out anywhere, and it's spring break so it's not like I'm required in classes.

I decide to tell my aunt what's going on. I leave out no details, and she listens completely before speaking.

"I'm proud of you, Sophia."

That's all she says.

Belle bites her bottom lip and leans toward the phone. "You're not mad?"

"As long as you're safe, I'm not mad. And honestly, Sophia, I think you're doing the right thing."

She doesn't have to explain herself. I know the hidden meaning behind her words has everything to do with my parents and not with me being a rebellious teenager. "Are you sure you're safe?"

"Yes," I say. "We're still on campus. We're just... hiding."

She chuckles. "Okay. Don't get into trouble. I expect you two to be back in your dorm in two days. And then I'll take you to a birthday dinner."

I grin. "Thanks Aunt Kate."

SOLAR POWERED LIGHTS cast a beautiful glow on the garden walls as the sun sets on our third day of this secret campout adventure. Declan's laptop plays our favorite Netflix comedy while we sit around eating pizza. Declan is the kind of guy I just like being around. I never get bored with him. It never feels weird. I'm not sure what our future holds, but I really hope we stay together. One of these days, I'll have to talk to him about it, but right now I just want to go with the flow. What we have is magical, and sweet, and fun. I don't want to ruin it by wondering what comes next.

Declan smells like cedar and something sweet, like cinnamon, as he sits next to me on the blankets we've spread out in the center of the garden. I lean against his chest, breathing him in and loving every second of being next to him.

"Are you going to tell us what's in that box?" I ask after the TV show is over and the credits roll on the computer. Earlier when Declan brought us dinner, he also brought a large box that's been sitting unopened for hours.

He glances at it and then gives me the cutest look. "Not yet."

"Why can't it be opened now?" I ask, gazing up at him while my head rests on his chest. "Is it some nerdy camping thing?"

He chuckles. "Nope."

Belle yawns. "You'll have to open it without me. I think I'm going to bed."

I turn on my phone to check the time. It's about fifteen minutes until midnight. "Goodnight."

"You sure you can't stay awake a little bit longer?" Declan asks her. "I don't want you to miss the surprise."

Belle shakes her head. "I have a pretty good idea of what it is. I'll see it in the morning." With one more yawn, she disappears into the tent and zips it closed.

"How does Belle know what's in the box and I don't?" I say, pointing an accusing finger at him.

Declan shrugs. "She doesn't know. She's guessing. I'm surprised you haven't guessed it."

"How would I guess something that's totally random?" I ask.

Declan kisses the top of my head and then turns back to the computer screen, which has started playing the next episode. "Guess you'll just have to wait and see."

I'm falling asleep on his shoulder when Declan whispers my name. "Wake up."

My eyes flit open and I yawn, stretching as I sit up on the blanket. The moonlight glows overhead. "Are you leaving? What time is it?"

"It's midnight," Declan says. "Which means it's time to open the box."

"Midnight?" Then I realize the significance behind the time. "It's my birthday"

I'm free. I made it four days and now my parents can't force me to leave.

"Yep," Declan says. He gets up and goes to the mysterious box. Inside, he pulls out a square white cardboard box.

I clap my hands together, recognizing the pink sticker label on the box. "You got me a cake! You are seriously the best boyfriend ever."

"I try," he says, handing me a plastic fork.

The cake is made of white icing that's covered in green and pink and purple icing flowers. Declan clearly had it custom made just for me, in a garden theme. "This is beautiful," I say, stabbing my fork in the corner to take a bite. "Thank you so much."

"There's... something more," he says with a nervous lilt in his voice. He reaches into the box and retrieves a much smaller box. Blue, with a silver ribbon tied around it.

My teeth dig into my bottom lip. "You got me a present..."

"I hope it's not weird," he says, looking more anxious

than I've ever seen him. "I know we haven't been together long but... you're special to me, Sophia."

With that, I know that whatever gift is inside here, I will cherish it forever. I open the box, and glance up at Declan. He's watching me nervously, which only makes me like him more.

"How did you get this?" I ask, picking up the beautiful silver necklace. It has a shiny silver charm that sparkles under the fairy lights. It's a key. A perfect replica of the real garden key, only it's small enough to be a necklace pendant.

"I had it custom made," he says, reaching out for the chain. "May I?"

I turn to the side and pull my hair back, letting him fasten the jewelry around my neck. My fingers wrap around the little key. "I love it," I whisper.

"Happy birthday," Declan says, kissing me gently on the lips.

I close my eyes and kiss him back. And I know two things: I will never ever take off this necklace. And this is the best birthday ever.

CHAPTER TWENTY-FOUR

"HOME SWEET HOME," Belle chimes as we enter our dorm room after four days of being pretend runaways. I mean, I guess we were kind of real runaways but it didn't feel like it. The outdoors is beautiful and I love our secret garden more than anything, but I'm happy to be home. We're coming home winners, as far as I'm concerned. I stuck it out, I'm an official adult, and I get to stay here until graduation. I might have lost a ton of money, but I'm slowly coming to terms with that.

It's early in the morning on my birthday, and I barely slept at all last night after Declan left. I keep reaching up and feeling my necklace, unable to hide my smile. I took the cake home and Belle and I plan on eating some for breakfast. I set the cake on my desk and then lug my backpack and suitcase into the closet and drop them on the floor. I'll clean out everything later. For now, I just want a nice hot shower, some cake, and a nap.

"Happy Birthday," Belle says. She's holding out a present wrapped in purple polka dot paper. Her smile reaches all the way across her face.

"Belle! You didn't need to get me anything."

She rolls her eyes. "You're my cousin and my bestie. I wanted to get you something."

My birthdays over the years have always been a big deal. As a kid, my parents would rent out some massive ballroom and fill it with princess stuff, a white horse, bounce houses, and more. As a teenager, my parents would let me rent out the coolest night club and invite all my friends and have a big dance party with mock-tails and lots of Justin Bieber music. The last few years have been kind of a contest between my Malibu friends and me as we all try to outdo each other with extravagant parties.

But this year, I'm celebrating with my boyfriend and my cousin on the campus of our school. I think this is my favorite birthday celebration yet.

I pull off the wrapping paper, revealing a shipping box. She's blacked over the label with a marker so I can't tell which company she ordered from, which makes it all the more mysterious. Inside the box, I pull out something bubble-wrapped. It looks a lot like a laptop cover. The kind that snaps over the top and bottom of it to protect it.

And that's exactly what it is. I bite my lip to hold back the tears as I reveal the custom photo laptop case Belle has ordered for me. I don't know when she took this picture, or how she took it because it's so stunning, it's basically professional quality. It's a photo of my garden.

"It's so you'll always remember it, you know, after you've graduated."

I press the laptop case to my chest and hug it. "I love it so much, thank you." Then I give her a coy grin. "But what makes you think I'm leaving?"

She blinks. "We have to leave. You said it yourself. We can't stay in these dorms forever."

"I know but... I don't want to leave this town. I'm thinking of asking Aunt Kate if I can move in with you guys after graduation. And maybe go to college around here."

"Really?"

I nod.

Belle grins. "We do have a spare bedroom."

"Do you think Aunt Kate would mind?"

"Are you kidding? She'd love it."

I take a deep breath. There are still a few weeks of school left. Still time to figure stuff out. I'm way behind on finding colleges, because for most of my senior year, I figured I'd just grow up and be a rich heiress with no education needed. But now I want college. I want a career I love, maybe even one in botany. I could be a florist. Or a landscaper. Maybe Declan and I could start our own company and take back the job from the contractor Shelfbrooke hired. A deep blush creeps into my cheeks at the thought.

It's way too early to be picturing my life with Declan, but it's fun to do it anyway.

"Whoa," Belle says, staring at her phone. "I just checked my school email and my Knight Watch..."

"What is it?" I reach for my phone.

"The dean is looking for you."

Chills race across my neck. I load my school email and see several messages, from Ms. Beverly at the front desk and then one from Dean Thomas himself. I click on it, not sure what to expect. It's not like I've ever met the man before.

Dear Ms. Brass,

Please visit me during my office hours at your earliest convenience.

Regards,

Dean Thomas

Belle reads over my shoulder. "Whoa."

"That sounds bad." I look up at her. "Is that bad? It's bad."

"It's probably not good," Belle agrees.

"I wonder if I'm expelled?"

"Maybe he has a birthday present for you," she says, trying and failing at making a joke. My heart is pounding too hard to laugh right now.

"Or maybe I'm in huge freaking trouble." I heave a sigh and open my closet, pulling out a Shelfbrooke uniform.

"What are you doing?" Belle asks.

"I'm going to go face my fate." My shower and nap and cake for breakfast will just have to wait. There's no way I could enjoy those things with this mysterious email from the dean hanging over my head. I tug on my uniform and brush my hair and give Belle a weak smile.

Then I walk to the front office.

Ms. Bev's blonde bun is tight and neatly tied on top of her head. She smiles warmly at me, and I wonder if it's just an act, or maybe she miles like this at everyone.

"I'm here to see the dean," I say, drumming my

fingers on the counter. "He, uh, emailed me asking me to stop by."

"Of course," she says, glancing at her computer. "I think he's free right now."

I walk on shaky legs as I step past the three chairs that sit just outside Dean Thomas' office. The door is mostly closed, the frosted glass panel making it impossible to see inside. I step up and knock lightly on the glass.

"Come in," a deep male voice says.

I swallow. I've never been to a real school before. I've always heard of the phrase 'getting sent to the principal's office' but I didn't realize how scary it would be to experience it in real life. Plus Dean Thomas is a dean, not a principal, and I'm pretty sure that makes this whole situation even scarier. If he kicks me out now, I'll have nowhere to go. My mom would just *love* it if I had to come crawling back to her.

The Dean is wearing a crisp suit with the Shelfbrooke Academy crest embroidered on his blazer. He's not terribly tall, but he has a commanding presence. His salt and pepper hair makes him look slightly older than he probably is.

"Ms. Sophia Brass, I assume?"

I swallow. "How did you know?"

I glance at his computer, but the screen is facing

away from me so I have no idea what it says. "You opened my email five minutes ago."

I nod and draw in a breath. "Good ol' email read receipts."

"Have a seat," he says. I drop into the chair across from his desk. The window behind him shows a picturesque view of the campus grounds. It feels mean to have such a beautiful sight in the office where I'm assuming a lot of students get handed punishments for breaking the rules.

Dean Thomas props his elbows on his desk, lacing his fingers together. He takes a long time to talk. I'm guessing it's some administration scare tactic they teach in graduate school.

"Ms. Brass, you've had quite an adventure lately."

"I have?" I say, because what else am I supposed to say?

He nods once. "I have never seen a student hide out in the gardens to avoid being taken out of this school."

Chills slither down my spine. "You knew?"

His smile makes him look... impressed?

"Of course," he says. He taps his keyboard. "All devices connected to the Shelfbrooke Wi-Fi have GPS capabilities, as well as student log in information. When your mother burst into my offices unannounced, accusing me of losing one of my own students because the student was not in her dorm room, I was concerned. I did a little research and found you and another student, your roommate, logged in and located somewhere in the gardens."

It feels like a knife has been shoved straight into my heart. He knew my location. He knows my secret garden. This is a nightmare.

"Why didn't you come get me?" I ask, my voice weak.

He chuckles. "Those gardens are huge. As long as you and your cousin were safe, I didn't see the reason to send a search party. The GPS is only accurate to within hundred meters, anyway."

"Oh." I breathe the biggest sigh of relief of my life. He doesn't know my garden. He didn't even come looking for me. "Thank you," I say, realizing these past few days could have gone a lot differently.

"You are quite welcome, Ms. Brass."

"Am I in trouble?" I ask.

"You have straight A's and nearly perfect attendance," he says. "Plus I hear you are taking good care of another student who has been confined to her room for three years. Your aunt has said nothing but great things about you. So no, you are not in trouble."

I burst into the biggest grin possible. "Thank you, sir."

"One more thing," he says, standing up and walking me to the door. "There are just a few weeks left of school. Please stay in your dorm and abide by curfew for the rest of them."

"Yes, sir," I say. "I will."

EPILOGUE

IT'S graduation day at Shelfbrooke Academy. Declan and I meet in the gardens right at dawn to watch the sunrise in our favorite place. I can't believe we've kept our secret romance a secret so well. Word on Knight Watch is that Chad Stokes got arrested for selling prescription pills. He lost his acceptance into Harvard, and now he's scrambling to do something with his life because his parent's money can only get him out of trouble so many times. I'd like to say that I feel sorry for him, but I don't.

The great thing about graduating high school is that we can all move on with our lives. The whole world is opened to us now.

"I kind of wish we weren't graduating," Declan says. We're sitting on a blanket on the plush grass of our garden, me leaning against his chest. He props himself up with one hand and runs the other hand through my hair.

"Why on earth would you say that?" I tease. "Getting out of high school is the best thing ever. And I only had to do it for a few months. I don't know how the rest of you survived four years of it."

He chuckles. "I'm going to miss the garden, that's all."

"Babe." I sit up and put my hands on his shoulders. "If you think I am above breaking and entering, you are so wrong."

His gorgeous face crinkles in confusion. "What?"

"I already have a plan, you see. You know that gate that leads to the street outside of campus?"

"Yes..."

I wiggle my eyebrows. "I shoved a piece of cardboard into the lock."

"What!" Declan's eyes are as blue as the tulips beside us. "Are you sure we can get away with this?"

I shrug. "It's just temporary. Until we both get summer jobs as gardeners. Then we can come and go as we please."

Declan sighs. "That's impossible, Sophia. The company only hired me because of my grandfather. Now that I'm graduating, my job is gone."

I shake my head. I've waited several days to be able to tell him this good news. I've been saving it for the perfect moment, and this feels like it.

My life has changed a lot in the last few weeks. My mom apologized, for one. She called me up and said she had met a new yoga teacher who made her realize that she'd been too harsh on me. She's still upset that I didn't want to be her pet perfect daughter in Africa, but she and I are on speaking terms again, which is a good thing. I do love my parents, even if they have different lives than I do.

And while I told my mom I didn't want my trust fund because I wanted to pursue my life on my own terms without the help of money, she wasn't having it. She said she'd earmark the money for me later in my life, when I'd "come around" as she put it, and want my inheritance again.

So I came up with a compromise.

I asked her to buy the landscaping contract for the gardens.

A few lawyer phone calls later, and Mom assured me it was done. Now my dad's company is in control of the school's famous gardens, and the first thing he's going to do is hire Declan's family back to run it full time.

I tell Declan the good news and he watches me in

awe, his jaw hanging open slightly. "Money really does solve a lot of problems," he says.

I laugh. "I hope you don't mind. I told them I'd like my inheritance in the form of a landscaping company. Dad said when I graduate college, he'll make me the VP of his newly formed company, Brass Landscaping,"

Declan's arm wraps around my waist. "So I'm going to be working for my girlfriend?" he says, grinning as he kisses my cheek.

"I was thinking we could run it together. Be like dual CEO's or something."

"Sounds fun," he says, leaning so close, I can feel his breath on my ear. "Now our garden can be ours forever."

I grin. "That's the plan."

Declan takes my face in his hands. The morning sunlight brings out the amber in his hair, and the sparkles in his eyes. "This place is magic," he says, tipping my face up until my lips meet his. "You are magic," he breathes against my lips.

A soft flutter in my heart makes me smile. I didn't know it was possible to be this happy.

We both turn as the soft sound of knocking interrupts our mushy love fest. "Sophia? Are you in here?" It's Belle's voice.

"Yes," I call out, scrambling to my feet. She'd been asleep when I left this morning.

The door opens up and my cousin steps into our garden, wearing her black and silver graduation gown. "I thought you'd be here."

"Did you walk here all by yourself?"

She nods. "I did. And I'm going to walk at graduation, too."

Belle has made a lot of progress lately. We walk up and down the hallway in our dorm every day, and we've gone outside a few times, too. We even passed by two students the other day and Belle didn't have an anxiety attack.

"Are you sure?" I ask. "We're going to be surrounded by people."

"Yes," Belle says confidently. "Because I've got this." She gestures to her graduation gown.

"Everyone will be wearing the same thing," Declan says in understanding.

"Yep," Belle agrees. "I'll be just another graduating student in a sea of other black and silver gowns. No one will notice me. And I'll be okay."

"I think we'll all be okay," I say.

Declan puts an arm around my shoulders. "I told you this place was magic."

ABOUT THE AUTHOR

Amy Sparling is the bestselling author of books for teens and the teens at heart. She lives on the coast of Texas with her family, her spoiled rotten pets, and a huge pile of books. She graduated with a degree in English and has worked at a bookstore, coffee shop, and a fashion boutique. Her fashion skills aren't the best, but luckily she turned her love of coffee and books into a writing career that means she can work in her pajamas. Her favorite things are coffee, book boyfriends, and Netflix binges.

She's always loved reading books from R. L. Stine's Fear Street series, to The Baby Sitter's Club series by Ann, Martin, and of course, Twilight. She started writing her own books in 2010 and now publishes several books a year. Amy loves getting messages from her readers and responds to every single one! Connect with her on one of the links below.

www.AmySparling.com

www.ingramcontent.com/pod-product-compliance
Ingram Content Group UK Ltd.
Pitfield, Milton Keynes, MK11 3LW, UK
UKHW042003190726
13854UKWH00005B/2144

9 798201 767402